The Wild Women of Lake Anna

A Bailey Fish Adventure

Also in the series:

No Sisters Sisters Club
Silver finalist, Florida Publishers Association,
Best Children's Fiction 2008

The Thief at Keswick Inn
President's Pick Award 2007
Florida Publishers Association

The Mysterious Jamestown Suitcase
Moonbeam Children's Book Award 2007
Bronze medalist

Gold medalist, Best Children's Fiction 2009
Florida Publishers Association

ForeWord magazine Book of the Year
finalist 2007

Ghost of the Chicken Coop Theater
Silver medalist, Best Children's Fiction 2009
Florida Publishers Association

Trouble in Contrary Woods

Captain Calliope and the Great Goateenies

Salisbury is also the author of
Mudd Saves the Earth
a humorous environmental book for kids.

The Wild Women of Lake Anna
A Bailey Fish Adventure

Linda Salisbury

**Drawings by
Christopher Grotke**

Tabby House

Third printing, 2010

Cover design: Carol Tornatore
Author photo: Ann Henderson
Illustrator photo: Paul Collins, courtesy of MuseArts

Library of Congress Cataloging-in-Publication Data

Salisbury, Linda G. (Linda Grotke)
  The wild women of Lake Anna : a Bailey Fish adventure
/ Linda Salisbury
     p. cm.
  Summary: Eleven-year-old Bailey Fish is abruptly sent
to live with her grandmother in Virginia, but she gains
courage from tales of her ancestral "wild women" and de-
cides to become one too.
  ISBN 1-881539-37-7
  [1. Moving, Household--Fiction. 2. Grandmothers--Fic-
tion. 3. Sex role--Fiction.] I. Title.
PZ7.S1524Wi2005
[Fic]--dc22

                              2004062061

Manufactured within CPSIA guidelines.
Printed by Sheridan Books, Inc.
Chelsea, Michigan
01/25/2010
Batch #1

Classroom quantities; teacher's guides available.

www.BaileyFish Adventures.com
BaileyFish@gmail.com

Tabby House
P.O. Box 544
Mineral, VA 23117
(540) 895-9093

Contents

1

Sugar

Bailey Fish slammed her small maroon carry-on suitcase on the green and yellow overstuffed chair in the guest bedroom. The thud it made pleased her but, fortunately, it wasn't loud enough for her grandmother to hear. Sugar, as Gram liked to be called, already had been forced to wait for forty-five minutes for Bailey's plane to arrive from Fort Myers, Florida. And then Bailey's big blue suitcase on wheels, filled with her favorite clothes, was missing and she wouldn't be able to get her things until tomorrow. That included the framed photos of her mother, Molly Fish, and Barker, her black cat that had been run over just after Christmas.

"Bailey, supper will be ready in about ten minutes," her grandmother called from the kitchen. "My very special mac and cheese."

Bailey didn't answer. She jerked on the zipper of the suitcase and it jammed. *Rats*, she thought. She decided to work on opening it later and instead walked to the dormer window and looked out.

It sure gets dark early in Virginia, thought Bailey as she stared into the tall woods behind the house. Nothing looked like home in Florida, where her bedroom was on the first floor, not upstairs.

Hot tears filled her hazel eyes. Why had her mother decided to travel without her to Costa Rica? She might be gone the rest of fifth grade or even longer. Sugar was okay, well, actually fun sometimes. But to live with her grandmother for a whole year? And so far from her friends in Florida?

Bailey threw a pillow across the room. It hit the wall next to the dresser and landed in a wastebasket. She picked it up and buried her face in it, letting a few tears escape.

"Supper's on," called Sugar. "Wash up and come on down, girl. We have some planning to do."

Bailey found the towels that didn't match that Sugar had set out for her, and washed her hands. She looked in the mirror and saw her red eyes, wiped them with the cool washcloth, pushed her straight, medium-brown hair behind her ears, then headed down the stairs.

Nothing matched in Sugar's kitchen either, including the dishes. Mom said that after Sugar had retired, she stopped at even more yard sales and Goodwill stores than ever before. She couldn't resist bargains.

"Sugar calls these trips 'treasure hunts,' and I'm sure she'll want you to go with her, honey," Molly said as she helped Bailey pack.

Bailey, who liked to buy clothes at the big mall, was worried. "But what if she makes me dress in stupid stuff she gets at yard sales, Mom? That would be awful."

Her mother didn't answer, but instead pressed twenty dollars into her hand. "Here, have some fun. Don't look so sad. We can call and e-mail and write. And you can e-mail your friend, Amber, too."

That was on Monday. By Wednesday, Bailey was on a plane, all by herself, feeling very little and alone. She had to sit up front with the small children, who were also flying by themselves. Even though the flight attendant offered all the kids extra boxes of cookies in the shape of airplanes, Bailey didn't feel better. She pretended to be asleep so she wouldn't have to talk with anyone.

How could her mother leave her, especially in the middle of the school year when she had just tried out for a class play and had been invited to Brook's birthday party? They had even bought Brook a present, a green T-shirt with pink and purple butterflies.

Sugar, wearing a heavy red-plaid jacket and brown slacks, waved when Bailey walked through the Jetway from the plane to the gate. She gave her one of the biggest hugs Bailey could ever remember getting from anyone. She had forgotten how good those Grandma hugs made her feel. Now that she was in Sugar's toasty kitchen filled with the scent of simmering apple sauce, Bailey realized that she was very hungry from traveling.

Sugar pretended not to notice her granddaughter's red eyes. She smiled as she looked at Bailey sitting at the kitchen table.

"Here, have some macaroni, garden beans, and homemade apple sauce. I like to serve it warm at this time of year. And I bought a chocolate cake for dessert. Tomorrow we'll get your big suitcase, and then we will have a treasure hunt on the way home," said Sugar.

When Sugar smiled, it was with the same big smile that her mother had. Bailey couldn't resist. She smiled, too. After she swallowed her third bite, Bailey said, "I've always wondered why we call you Sugar instead of Grandma?"

"It's because I'm so sweet," said Sugar, in a fake gruff voice, "and it keeps me from sounding as old as someone who is a grandma. You know, if you and I hang out together, people might think we are sisters." She peered at Bailey over her glasses.

Bailey had to laugh at that one.

"And you really like living here in the woods so far from everybody?" she asked

"Sure do. It's peaceful. I can sing out loud and nobody complains," said Sugar. She moved her glasses even lower on her nose and raised her eyebrows three times to make Bailey smile.

Bailey noticed that Sugar had more crinkles in her soft, round face than the last time she had seen her, but they were mostly around her eyes and the corners of her mouth, helping make her smiles look really huge.

This was the first time Bailey had been to Sugar's house in the country. Sugar had sent pictures of it when she moved in, but the house seemed so much bigger than in the snapshots. The yellow siding and green trim made the house stand out from the tall trees around it.

As Bailey had carried her suitcase up the front steps, she had noticed a porch swing and some flowerpots with dried plants remaining from last summer. A small, greenish-brown metal boat on a trailer was parked in the side yard. *The boat is the color that soldiers wear*, thought Bailey.

"I didn't know you had a boat," said Bailey, as she helped herself to more apple sauce sprinkled with ground cinnamon and cloves.

"I bought it a few years ago. It's pretty easy for one person to manage," said Sugar. "I like to take a picnic supper out on the lake. We could do that sometime, if you like picnics."

"I love picnics," said Bailey. She remembered how her mother packed whatever they were having for supper along with paper plates and plastic forks and knives in a basket, and off they went to watch the sunset at Gilchrist Park. They spread out supper on a wooden table, not worrying if the food was now cold. Sometimes they tossed leftover pieces of bread to the sea gulls, just as the sun went down. Her mother never planned the picnics more than five minutes in advance. It made them much more fun that way.

Just then the phone rang. Bailey hoped it was her mother, but instead it was a call from one of Sugar's friends. As Bailey continued to eat, she looked out the dark kitchen window near the table. She was surprised to see a face, a man with a long beard and stringy hair. Before she could open her mouth to yell, he disappeared as quickly as he had come. Bailey was about to take another bite of macaroni when she saw the face again.

"Sugar, look!" Bailey waved her fork at the window. "Look!"

But Sugar was pacing around the kitchen with the phone. She briefly stared in the direction Bailey was pointing, but was too engrossed in her conversation to let anything interrupt it. She said to the caller, "What? Not again! We'll get to the bottom of this!"

Bailey was surprised at how upset her grandmother sounded.

Sugar listened for awhile, then said, "Okay, okay." As she hung up the phone she asked, "Did you say something, Bailey?"

Bailey wasn't sure if she should mention the face. Maybe it wasn't real and her grandmother would think she was making things up. Instead she asked, "What was all that about?"

"There are more signs of illegal dumping near Contrary Creek. Whatever is being dumped there contains chemicals that may pollute the water and kill the bass in Lake Anna," said Sugar.

"Contrary Creek? That's a funny name," said Bailey.

"I suppose. You know, there used to be mines for copper, iron, pyrite and even gold near Contrary Creek years ago," said Sugar.

"Gold? Real gold?" Bailey imagined big shiny gold nuggets spread out like rocks along the banks of a creek.

"Long time ago. There hasn't been much mining for years. But some people say they still find bits of gold in their yards, especially when they are building a house. I never have though," said Sugar. "And there are people who still pan for gold around here in the creek bed," she added.

"Now I've got to make some phone calls tonight, after you get settled in," said Sugar. "But first, let's get things cleaned up. I'll wash and you dry." She handed Bailey a frayed blue terry cloth dish towel.

"And I need to show you around the house so you know where everything is and where to find books. I know you like to read," she said.

The old house didn't look very big from the outside, but indeed, there were a number of rooms added by different owners. Sugar had an office near her bedroom on the first floor, a living room with several big chairs, a couch, and a fireplace. Each side table was piled high with books and papers, not like those at her mother's house, which was very neat. Sugar also had a back porch for reading once the weather was warm enough.

Later, as Bailey slid between a red sheet on the top and blue striped one on the bottom, she heard an owl. The mournful *hu hu hu* was loud for a few minutes, then faded as the owl flew farther into the woods.

She remembered the scary face in the window. *I must be imagining things,* thought Bailey. When she stayed home alone in Florida, Bailey always believed she heard voices or someone outside a window but when she told her mother, Molly would laugh. Then her mom always said, "You're a silly goose. Stop being such a worrier. Nobody will bother you as long as the doors are locked."

Bailey did keep the doors locked, but the creaking sounds still made her jump sometimes.

If a bad man was really there, Sugar would have noticed, wouldn't she? Bailey wondered, as she wrapped her arms around her pillow and closed her eyes.

2

First Treasure Hunt

With the big blue suitcase safely strapped in the back of Sugar's red pickup truck, Bailey felt a little more ready for adventure. The people at the Richmond airport said they were sorry that Sugar had to make the special trip back for it. Bailey was glad to collect her luggage so she could get her clothes unpacked. As they left the parking lot, she remembered that her grandmother had said something about a mysterious treasure hunt on the way home. Once the pickup turned north on Route 522, Sugar said, "Now watch for a sign on the right."

"What kind of sign?" asked Bailey.

"Oh, just the first sign that has something you think you might want," said Sugar, with that crinkly smile that made everyone, including Bailey, feel happier.

Bailey peered out the window as the truck sped along the hilly, curvy roads. There were very few houses and lots of farmland. Bailey saw black cows and a shaggy brown pony. Some fields had bales of hay or straw that were rolled up like the shredded wheat biscuits that her mother liked to eat.

It certainly wasn't like Florida with houses close together and lots of traffic and red lights that always made her mother mad.

She saw signs advertising firewood and others advertising farms for sale. Then as they neared Apple Grove, Bailey said, "There! Stop there!" Sugar smiled again. A brown board was propped against a tree near the side of the road. It had these big red words: FREE KITTENS ONE-HALF MILE.

"Do you really mean I can have a kitten?"

"You can have two," said her grandmother, "so long as you take care of them. But that is assuming you find two that you like."

"I'm sure I will," said Bailey, feeling a little less homesick. She had been responsible for her sweet fat cat, Barker, when he was alive. She fed, combed him—when he let her—and sometimes cleaned the litter box. Barker had always run to the door when Bailey came home and had curled up in her lap while she read.

Her throat still ached when she thought about how much she missed him.

Sugar knocked on the front door of the brick house at the end of a long, dirt driveway. A tall woman wearing a gray sweatshirt and blue jeans led them down a hallway to her kitchen.

"I just put the sign out yesterday," she said. "You are the first people to stop by."

The kittens—six of them—were eight weeks old and none was the same color. Bailey sat on the floor near a cardboard box where they tumbled in and out. How could she decide? Sugar pulled up a chair at the wooden kitchen table and talked with the woman who was stroking Looloo, the mother tabby cat.

The woman said she hoped it would be an early spring. She wanted to get her peas planted, but the forecast had been for near-freezing weather for the next few weeks, and for more rain.

Bailey studied all the kittens and moved her hand in circles on the floor to watch them play.

She finally decided on a black-and-white kitten with long hair and soft paws because it reminded her of Barker. When it jumped on a silky gray one and they rolled and rolled together, Bailey knew they were a pair.

The tall woman gave Bailey a small sack of kitten chow and enough litter to get them set up at Sugar's house.

"I can see that they will have a really good home," the woman said. Bailey held the kittens in the cardboard carton punched with holes as Sugar's pickup headed back up the highway.

The little paws sticking out of the holes made Bailey laugh as the truck went past a place called Cuckoo, through Mineral and to the lake area where Sugar lived.

"Have you come up with names?" Sugar asked.

"The gray one is Shadow; the other is Sallie," said Bailey.

"Good names," said Sugar. "If they don't tear up the curtains, they can sleep in your room tonight. They will probably be missing their mother, too."

Bailey rubbed their soft ears and heads through the holes. Sallie stuck her paw out of one.

"We'll need to get some cat toys, like those little mice with rattles," said Sugar. "Kittens always like to play with things."

"I made Barker a toy once. It was a piece of paper on a string tied to a stick. He jumped all over the place," said Bailey. "It was crazy."

"I think I have string and a stick," said Sugar. "And there's always plenty of paper at my house, as I'm sure you've noticed."

Shadow licked Bailey's finger as she wiggled it inside the box.

Maybe having adventures with Sugar isn't so bad after all, Bailey thought, *especially one with kittens.*

3

Florida Girl

"I'll only be gone a few minutes," said Sugar. "My cell phone number is written down on that pad on the counter right by the telephone—if you need me. I've got to talk with my friend, Harry, about the dumping, and then, when I get back, we'll go to Mineral."

Bailey heard the phone ring after she had gone to bed last night. She couldn't understand what Sugar was saying, but at times her voice was loud and she spoke fast. Bailey figured it had something to do with the pollution.

She was surprised that Sugar was going off without her, but when Sugar asked, "Are you sure you don't mind staying home alone?" all Bailey said was, "I'll be fine. I *am* eleven."

Home. That still sounded funny. Home should be in Florida. But the house where she and Molly had lived since Bailey was in second grade was going to be rented out while they were both away. Home was with Sugar— at least for now.

After playing much too much during their first night in Bailey's room, Shadow and Sallie had collapsed next to each other on the couch. Bailey decided not to tell Sugar that the kittens woke her up three times with their games because she wanted them to keep her company at night.

Rather than disturb them, Bailey decided to look around the yard while Sugar was gone. A few green shoots had pushed their way through the clammy reddish-yellow soil. It was so different from the gray sandy yards of Florida. There were no palm trees or hibiscus or prickly pink bougainvillea in the yard. Sugar's big trees had a few buds but no leaves. It was too early for spring.

The chilly, damp air seemed to go right through her lavender, hooded sweatshirt. She put her hands in its pockets. *Virginia sure is cold*, she thought as she walked down the gravel driveway to the road.

As she neared the mailbox, she saw a boy about her age with his back to her. His bike was on the ground near him. He had dark hair that looked like it hadn't been washed since he was born. It also needed cutting.

"Hey," she said, trying to sound friendly.

The boy turned abruptly, dropping the butt of a cigarette he had been trying to light. He gave her a hard look, picked up the butt and put it in the torn pocket of his gray jacket.

"What are you doing here?" he demanded with a sneer. "You shouldn't go around surprising people."

"I live here," said Bailey, wishing she had stayed in the house.

The boy's scruffy brown dog, with one ear up and the other half-chewed, stood behind him. Both glared at her.

"Who are you?" he asked coldly.

"Bailey Fish."

The boy didn't say anything, but just looked her over. Then he said slowly, "So I heard. That's a dumb name."

Bailey couldn't think of anything to say. Nobody had ever said that to her before.

"Cat got your tongue?" asked the boy. "Just so you know, I'm Justin Rudd." He turned his head and spit. "The Rudds have lived here a long, long time and we don't like new people. Newbies get in our way. They want to change everything."

Bailey remained silent.

Justin took a step closer to her. "Where you from BaileyFish?" He said her name like it was all one word, a word he didn't like.

"Florida. I just moved here," she said, stepping back.

"You—I hear you live with your grandma, BaileyFish. That's what my dad says."

"Yeah, for awhile," she said.

"What's the matter, Florida girl? No mother or father? Or don't they like you around, Florida girl?"

The back of Bailey's eyes stung and her throat felt tight. She didn't want this awful boy to see her cry, so she bit the inside of her cheek to stop the tears, something she had done since she was very little.

She really wanted to run but instead put her hands on her hips and stuck out her chin. "None of your business," she said as bravely as she could. But she didn't feel brave around this mean boy or his dog. The dog looked like he would bite her if Justin told him to.

The boy unwrapped a stick of gum, dropped it in his mouth then threw the wadded paper into Sugar's driveway.

"Well, BaileyFish, this ain't Florida, as you'll see. Besides, my daddy says your grandma is an old busybody bag. She's always snooping around stuff. He says he'd like to fix her wagon for getting him in trouble with the law. So, you'd better watch out, BaileyFish. And your grandma, too," said Justin.

He spit again, then tossed a stick for the dog and started down the hill on his bike. The sun disappeared behind a large white cloud.

Bailey shivered.

She opened the mailbox and gathered the long white envelopes. She looked for something with her name on it, but all of them were addressed to her grandmother. One was marked "urgent."

Bailey took one last look down the road. Justin and his nasty-looking dog were gone.

"Good riddance," she said, as she picked up the gum wrapper to put in Sugar's trash can.

She hoped there were kids besides Justin in the neighborhood. Sugar hadn't mentioned if there was anybody her age nearby, and Bailey hadn't thought to ask.

Bailey put the envelopes on the kitchen counter near the toaster and decided to wake Shadow and Sallie. She hoped they would warm her cold hands and make her forget that terrible boy.

4

E-mail for Bailey

Sugar scowled as she opened the mail. The letter marked "urgent" contained a laboratory report on the pollution. It was based on water samples that she and her friend Harry Smith collected two weeks earlier.

"This doesn't look good. We've got to find out what is going on," Sugar said. "Toxic materials are leaching—that means spreading—from an illegal landfill in someone's yard, and getting into a stream that goes into Contrary Creek and eventually the lake. It seems to be getting worse lately."

Sugar seemed to be talking to herself, but Bailey listened carefully. When she lived in Florida, Bailey had done a school project about different types of water pollution. And she remembered how stinky the beaches smelled when fish died during algae blooms called red tide.

She remembered that one Sunday she and her mother were enjoying a picnic at Englewood Beach until the wind shifted and suddenly everyone started to cough and sneeze. The smell of rotting fish was so bad that they finally went home. Although scientists were not completely sure what caused red tide, Bailey learned that some thought it might be pollution. Whatever the reason, red tide and pollution were not good for the birds, or fish and other creatures that live in the water. Bailey received an A on her report and won an honorable mention in the district science fair.

As soon as Sugar finished reading her mail, she said, "So how was your morning? I'm sorry I was gone longer than I thought."

Bailey wanted to tell her about meeting Justin Rudd, but Sugar didn't give her a chance. "Let's check the e-mail," she said. "Maybe there will be something for you."

Sugar booted up the computer, an old slow one, and clicked on the envelope icon on the bottom of the screen. The e-mail messages were displayed.

Sure enough, along with a number of e-mails for Sugar, there were two for Bailey, one from her mother, and one from her best friend, Amber.

From: mollyf2@travl.net
To: "Sugar" <sugarsugarr@earthluv.net>
Sent: Wednesday 11:15 PM
Subject: For Bailey

My dearest Bailey: How I miss you! The plane ride to Costa Rica was pretty bumpy—you wouldn't have liked it at all. I was met at the airport in San Jose by Manuel, my driver. We headed into the mountains, near Volcano Arenal, where I will be staying and working and doing some of my research for awhile.
I hope you are having wonderful adventures with Sugar. Be sure to help her with housework and the dishes. Got to go. I only have a few minutes to use the computer we all share at the lodge.
Love and kisses, Mom

And from Amber:

From: jbs25@yermail.net
To: "Sugar" <sugarsugarr@earthluv.net>
Sent: Thursday 7:04 PM
Subject: To Bailey

I really miss you.
What's Virginia like? Have you met any new
friends yet? Mom said I can take gymnastics this
summer. Write back. Your friend, Amber

Bailey told both of them about her new kittens and that Sugar was trying to stop a polluter. Then to Amber she added:

I met a really horrible boy on a bike. He made
fun of me. Virginia's OK, but he isn't. His name
is Justin Rudd, but I'm going to call him Justin
Rude. I miss you, too. Best friends forever, Bailey.

Sugar called from the other room, "Tomorrow I'll set you up with your own e-mail address, but for now log off and grab a jacket. We're going to town."

5

A Spy in the Family

"You know, you come from a family of Wild Women," said Sugar as she drove along the country roads on their way to town.

Bailey studied the countryside. Besides the rolling hills, deep woods, and occasional glimpses of the creeks flowing into Lake Anna, she saw that in some places loggers had cleared the land of trees, leaving felled trunks, and stumps with their roots upturned.

"Wild Women?" asked Bailey as she wondered if new trees would ever be planted in the fields with dead ones.

"Yes. My aunt, Mae, your great-great-aunt, was a spy during World War I. That's what we've heard about her anyway. She went to France and Spain, as part of her job as a buyer for Macy's Department Store in New York. She was looking at all the latest fashions in Europe, but while she was there, she carried secret messages in code from our government. The enemy didn't suspect her because she was elegant and very clever," said Sugar.

"Wow, a real spy! I didn't even know we had a spy in our family. I didn't know I had any great-greats," said Bailey. "Mom and I watched a video about a lady spy. Did Great-great-Aunt Mae wear a costume?"

"I guess she dressed fancy so they wouldn't notice secret activities. Maybe she had a veil to cover her face. There's a picture of her on the wall in your bedroom. I'll show you when we get back," said Sugar. "Aunt Mae was very beautiful with her red hair and green eyes. She had many lovely hats, including a little one with a small feather."

"Really?" said Bailey trying to remember.

"You can't see the feather very well, but it is there. There is a little pocket in the hat brim where she hid the messages." Then Sugar whispered, "And I have that hat."

"You do?" Bailey's eyes grew large. "Can I see it?"

Sugar nodded.

"Did you or Mom ever want to be a spy, Sugar?" asked Bailey.

"You bet! I'm sort of a spy on that pollution problem we're investigating. Which reminds me, you've got to keep what you hear me talking about with Harry and others a secret. Promise?"

"I promise, but I don't even know anybody to tell," said Bailey. "The only person I've met so far is a rude boy named Justin Rudd, and his dog."

"When did you meet him? You didn't tell me that," said Sugar with a hint of worry in her voice.

Bailey squirmed. "This morning. He was riding his bike down the street and made fun of me living with you and not with my parents."

"Hmm," said Sugar, frowning. She pushed her sunglasses higher on her nose and ran her hand through her short, wavy, dyed-brown hair.

"Do you know him?" asked Bailey as the pickup slowed at a crossroad to let a tractor enter the highway.

"Yes, I know the family. Justin's father is pretty hard on the kids. They can never please him. Justin is the oldest of three or four, I think. And although the father has enough money, he doesn't take good care of his family.

"I will say that I've seen Justin look after his little sisters, even if he does act mean to other kids. I doubt that he is all bad, but he has a temper and a reputation of being a bully. Don't let him get to you, and try to stay out of his way if you can," said Sugar.

"Okay, but I don't like him," said Bailey. "Did you ever have a fight with his father?"

"Sort of, why?" asked Sugar.

"That's what Justin said, and he said something about his father wanting to get even," said Bailey. "He sounded like he meant it."

"Well, it's a long story," said Sugar. "His father has never forgiven me for calling animal control for what he was doing to his dogs a number of months ago. I saw him whipping one poor animal because it jumped out of the back of his truck. When the officers investigated, they saw animals that were chained and not very well cared for. So they took them away from him. There was a big story in the paper. He got mad and said that I would pay."

"What did he mean by that?" asked Bailey. "Is he going to hurt you?"

"I think he was just bluffing. I'm not terribly concerned. The sheriff is a friend of mine. He stops by to check on me from time to time, so don't you worry," said Sugar.

Bailey wondered if she should mention the face in the window, but Sugar said, "Hey, we're coming into town now—Mineral."

"Gee, it's not like Port Charlotte," said Bailey as she stared out the window.

"Hardly. No McDonald's. No big stores, but we can get what we need for the kittens at the market, and something for supper, too. Then I will stop at the post office and the bank."

As they drove, Bailey looked at the few brick buildings, the gray railroad station, an abandoned school, churches and the gas station at the main intersection with its one traffic light. This was a town? Where would she get clothes and school supplies?

As if reading her mind, Sugar said, "Some day soon we'll go to one of the cities to do more shopping. Mineral is great for little things and to meet people. It's a place to find out what's going on and to swap news. You can't really judge a town by its stores," she said. "Now be thinking about what you would like for supper and what kind of food we should get for Shadow and Sallie."

Bailey remembered reading a book about traveling back in time and wondered if that was happening to her now. The town seemed really old.

Sugar said, "More than 100 years ago Mineral was a thriving mining town, with thousands of people living here. That's when they changed the name from Tolersville to Mineral—because of the mines."

"What happened to all the people?"

"When the mining ended, the workers went elsewhere to look for jobs. Now there are only about 450 people living in town," said Sugar.

"I think that's the size of my school at home," said Bailey.

As they loaded their brown grocery bag with kitten chow and a chicken Sugar planned to roast for supper into the truck, Bailey saw Justin Rudd glaring at her from a big, green car filled with kids. The dented car with a large, tired-looking woman behind the wheel screeched into the market's parking lot and stopped near Sugar's truck.

As her grandmother drove away, Bailey looked back and saw Justin carefully help one of his little blond sisters out of the rear seat while his mother went ahead of them into the store. He bent down and retied her shoelaces before taking her hand.

I still don't like him, thought Bailey.

6

The Wild Women

"What about the other Wild Women?" Bailey asked Sugar on the way home. She had been thinking about Mae and her hat the entire time her grandmother was in the post office.

"Well, my mother, your great-grandmother, was an adventurer. She climbed Mount Washington, went to Africa on safari, and drove a dog sled in Alaska once. I think that's pretty wild for a woman back then," said Sugar. "Most women worked in their houses, raising their families. They didn't go off on adventures around the world like she did."

"Was she a spy, too?"

"Not that we know of, but she was a science teacher and she kept specimens in jars in her cellar. Scared me half to death when I was a child, to see little dead things floating in glass jars. I had to look at them every time I took the laundry down to the wringer washer in the basement or was sent to get a jar of jam from her shelves near the furnace."

"Little things like what?" asked Bailey.

"Like dead snakes and baby mice without fur," said Sugar, making a spooky face.

"Yuck!" said Bailey.

"That's what I said. Yuck! But I always looked at them anyway. Imagine what it would have been like to be in her classes and have her come in with those little jars." Sugar chuckled.

"That would be really yucky," said Bailey.

"And she had a reputation as a wild driver. Everybody in town got out of her way when they saw her coming down the road, usually on the wrong side. She was wild, all right. She liked adventures."

"Did you ever go on any rides with her?"

"You bet. That's where I learned about treasure hunts and things you might find when you least expect it," said Sugar.

"So, you and my mother are also Wild Women?" asked Bailey as she opened the gingersnaps that Sugar bought for the ride home.

"Oh my, yes. We both love adventure. We're ready to pick up and go on a minute's notice.

Pack our bags and go whenever adventure calls," said Sugar.

"That's what Mom did, isn't it?" Bailey's voice sounded sad.

Sugar looked at her granddaughter. Out of the corner of her eye, she watched Bailey twist the brown hair she had pushed behind her ears. Bailey's sweater was worn and too small. She hadn't come north with the clothes she needed for the cooler Virginia weather. She needed more jeans and sweatshirts, a warm jacket and maybe a new pair of shoes. Her shorts, sandals and T-shirts were fine for hot summer days, but the air was often cool at night, much cooler than Bailey was accustomed to in Florida.

They needed to shop soon before she enrolled Bailey in school. She knew that it would be hard for Bailey to start over in a new school in the middle of the year. Most kids would already have made best friends and they were used to their teachers. The material being taught might not be the same. Sugar sighed.

"Sometimes having an adventure means leaving the people you love for a little while," said Sugar. "Usually home seems so much better when you return. That's a part of having an adventure.

"Now I thought you'd want to know about mine. I've had too many to tell you about between now and when we get back to the house, but I've ridden in a blimp. I've gone deep-sea diving and once I rode an elephant in a circus, and floated in a hot air balloon," said Sugar.

"And I drove across country all by myself when I was just out of college. Here's our turn. And pass those gingersnaps, young lady. They are for both of us, you know, even if they are not on my diet."

Bailey stopped twisting her hair and smiled.

As they came to Sugar's driveway, Sugar stopped the truck and said, "What on earth?"

Someone had dumped garbage all around the mailbox. Empty cereal boxes, milk containers, beer bottles, chicken bones, and dirty diapers spilled out from torn plastic sacks.

"Who would do that?" Sugar muttered. "I guess we've got some cleaning up to do."

7

New Worries

Bailey, wearing her warm, blue flannel pajamas and fuzzy yellow slippers, padded into the kitchen. She trailed a stick with a long string and wadded piece of newspaper tied to the end. The kittens ran right behind, slipping and sliding on the linoleum as they tried to catch the paper "bird." She flicked the paper in the air, and both kittens stretched their paws and jumped as high as they could.

The kittens were lots of fun. Shadow and Sallie curled up with her each night, one on her neck and the other by her left ear. Bailey's fingers would find their soft bellies and they stretched and rolled. She stroked them in the morning until it was time to get up. They liked to be rubbed on the head, and nuzzled her if she stopped, even for a second.

Her grandmother was having her second cup of coffee as she studied a map spread out on the pine table. The kitchen smelled like burnt toast. Sugar often got busy reading or doing crossword puzzles and forgot that she was cooking.

"What are you looking at, Sugar?" asked Bailey as she poured round oats into a bowl. She felt less afraid to ask questions now than she had been during the first few days at her grandmother's house.

"A map of Louisa County," said Sugar. "We have an idea where the pollution is coming from—the general area, at least. Harry and I are planning to walk around some land over here," she said, pointing to a thin blue line, a stream, that emptied into Contrary Creek. See this darker line? It comes out down our street. It's an old road used first by the gold miners and now by the loggers and hunters."

"Are you allowed to go there?" asked Bailey.

"I know the owner, but because I'm not sure if he's the one involved, I guess we'll have to do some trespassing," said Sugar, "to check it out. Then if we find the evidence, we'll call the authorities."

"That sounds dangerous," said Bailey, worried. Sugar was all she had left at the moment.

If something happened to her, then what? Where would she live? Her heart felt like it was in her throat.

"Don't you worry. Harry's wife, Alice, will come stay with you while we go tramping around some evening. We have it all planned, and we have our signals. Alice knows what to do if there is any trouble," said Sugar.

Bailey wanted to ask what kind of trouble, but Sugar was busy writing something on a yellow legal pad. When she was done, she folded the paper and put it in her pocket.

Bailey suddenly didn't like living in a family of Wild Women. She wished her mother and grandmother were like other people's. She wished that they didn't like adventures quite so much. Then her mother would stay home, and her grandmother wouldn't get into trouble.

"And we have something to do today," continued Sugar. "We need to go to Fredericksburg to shop for school things. Now that you've gotten settled in, I need to enroll you in your classes. Your break is over."

Bailey's stomach churned. Going to school probably meant seeing Justin Rudd everyday, maybe even riding on the bus with him.

"Can't I just stay home with you?" she asked. "You could get homework for me and

I'd just do it." No longer hungry, Bailey stirred the banana slices around and around in her cereal.

Sugar said firmly, "The more you learn in school, the better your adventures will be. Remember your great-great-aunt and your great-grandmother became teachers. Mae wouldn't have been as good a spy if she hadn't learned to speak several languages. All of us Wild Women read lots of books. That reminds me, we need to get you a library card."

Bailey did love to read. In fact, reading had been her best subject back home at Liberty Elementary School. She much preferred curling up with a book to watching television shows, even the ones her friends liked. Since she had been at Sugar's house, she had almost finished the book on Thomas Edison that she had brought with her. And, as she had explored her grandmother's house, Bailey discovered Sugar had a large collection of books, including some from her childhood. There was an entire set of the Oz books, and six from the Little Maid series about girls growing up in different parts of the country many years ago. There were Dr. Doolittle and Freddie the Pig books, *Heidi,* and at least ten Nancy Drew mysteries, plus *A Wrinkle in Time,* the complete set of *The Boxcar Children, Where the Red Fern Grows,* and *The Secret Garden.* Sugar had told Bailey that she could read any book she liked, but just to put it back when she was done.

"I didn't know there were a bunch of Oz books besides the one about the wizard," said Bailey. "I think I'll read them first."

"I'll be ready in about half an hour," said Sugar. "Fredericksburg has some big malls and the kind of stores you like."

8

Sugar Makes a Deal

Bailey's new school clothes—three pairs of jeans, a green plaid long-sleeved shirt, three turtlenecks, a warm gray jacket with pink trim, brown leather shoes—her new notebooks and pencils were laid out on a table in her bedroom. Shadow and Sallie had already found the pile very comfortable for napping. They were curled up in the center of it.

Bailey had to admit that her room was starting to look less like a guest room and more like her own. In an Oreo cookie tin on her dresser were pieces of a blue egg, which had fallen from a nest, and two red feathers from Sugar's yard. Next to it she had set up the pictures of her mother and Barker. On her bedside table with a lamp were three paperbacks that Sugar let her select at a bookstore in

Fredericksburg and best of all, on her bed was a new patchwork quilt.

It wasn't exactly a *new* quilt. When Bailey and Sugar were on one of their treasure hunts, they stopped at a yard sale near Culpeper. Sugar decided the quilt, with lots of red, white and blue squares, some striped and some with patterns, would brighten up Bailey's room. To her own surprise, Bailey agreed. The two of them examined the tiny stitches that the quilter had used to make it.

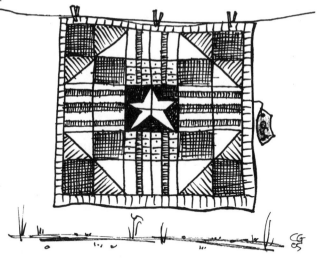

"It's an heirloom piece," whispered Sugar. "If you like it, let me see what they'll take for it. Just don't look like you want it. We need to act like we really don't care if they accept our offer," she said.

Bailey nodded and walked over to the next table filled with candles, jelly glasses, plastic dishes, picture frames, and baby clothes. She pretended not to be interested as Sugar offered the couple $25 for the quilt, which had a $50 price tag on it.

A man with a mustache and baseball cap with the words GONE FISHING on it said, "You've got to be kidding. That quilt is handmade." He sounded insulted. Instead of answering, Sugar walked over to the baby clothes and held up a little pink sleeper.

The man consulted with his wife, a short woman with thick, red hair.

"Okay, $40," he said after a minute.

Bailey was sure Sugar would say yes.

"Too much," said Sugar, not even looking at the quilt. "I'll give you $30, and that's my final offer. I saw a corner that needs repair." Bailey's heart sank. The quilt would have looked so pretty in her room.

She saw the couple conferring again. The sign down the road said the sale ended at three P.M. and it was now 2:45. As she and Sugar had driven up the driveway it looked like the couple was packing up large boxes with items from the tables. Perhaps they hadn't expected more customers and wanted to close early. But

Bailey figured they weren't going to lower the price. To her surprise, the woman said, "Well, all right. You've got yourself a deal."

Sugar and Bailey smiled at each other as they hurried away and heard the woman mutter to her husband, "Got more than we thought for that old thing."

After Sugar started the truck she said, "That's how it's done, Bailey. Never pay full price when you can bargain. The sellers expect it. It makes it more of an adventure. And this is a handsome spread. After we wash it, the quilt will look lovely on your bed."

Bailey started out being embarrassed by her grandmother's dickering, but then was proud of her when Sugar obtained the quilt at a lower price, especially when she said it was a beauty, an heirloom.

"You just never know what you'll find on these treasure hunts," Sugar said.

The quilt, freshly washed and dried outside on the clothesline, was perfect on the bed. Bailey especially liked the big white star in the center.

* * *

It was time to decide which of her new clothes to wear first. Bailey was not looking forward to starting school. She wondered what her teachers would be like and if any of the kids would be friendly. Or would they all be like Justin Rudd, making fun of her and her name. Would it be hard to find her way around the building? Would they have lockers and a band?

"Bailey, you're such a worrier," her mother used to say. But worrying was something that you couldn't help if you were a worrier.

Bailey sat on the floor petting Sallie and Shadow as they slept on her new blue sweater. She knew that Sugar was trying very hard to make her feel at home, but it wasn't the same as being in her own room in Florida and going to Liberty with her friends. She wondered if Amber missed her as much as she missed Amber. Amber with the freckles and blue eyes, who had the best secrets of anybody. Amber, who loved to dance and do tumbling. Amber, who liked to sleep over and watch *Finding Nemo* three times on a rainy day. Amber, who liked to make peanut butter and Marshmallow Peep sandwiches just to hear Bailey say, "Gross."

9

Homesick

From: "Bailey" <baileyfish@gmail.com>
To: jbs25@yermail.net
Sent: Tuesday 5:52 PM
Subject: To Amber

Hey Amber: I started school on Monday. Mrs.
Dudlee is nice enough. Some boys call her Mrs.
Dog Face. I have her for home room and lan-
guage arts. She put me in the advanced group. I
met Beth and Emily. They live near Sugar and are
showing me around the school. We might get
together this weekend if Sugar says OK. I saw
Justin Rude again when I was getting the mail.
He shouted Florida girl as he went by and asked
if my mother wanted me back yet. I hate him. I
also signed up for band. Has Skippy learned how
to beg? I miss you. Bailey

After Bailey sent the e-mail to Amber, she
saw there was a new one from her mother.
Bailey read it twice, hoping that her mother

would say either that she was coming home or that Bailey would be able to join her. As usual, her mom sounded very cheerful and there was no mention of coming back.

From: mollyf2@travl.net
To: "Bailey" <baileyfish@gmail.com>
Sent: Sunday 11:25 PM
Subject: Hiya

Bailey: You must have started school by now. I want to hear all about it. Has Sugar been behaving herself? I can see and hear the volcano erupt from the village where I'm staying. There are wild parrots and howler monkeys in the trees. We plan to go to the Pacific coast for a week. I hear there are beaches crawling with hermit crabs—just like the crabs you had in your second-grade class. I hear the kittens are quite lively. Ask Sugar to e-mail me a picture of you with them. Love, and kisses, Mom

Bailey typed a quick reply. She was glad that her mother had showed her how to use the computer so that they could write each other while she traveled. The day before Bailey left for Virginia, her mother downloaded eleven pages about Costa Rica. There were many pictures, including one of the volcano, and several maps of cities. Molly tried to show her where she would be staying, but Bailey didn't want to look at anything that day. She had to pack and try to call her friends to say good-bye. She put the papers in her suitcase without glancing at them. Her mother had seemed really happy about the trip, but Bailey wasn't. Why should she be?

Bailey logged off. Sugar had promised to take her out in her twelve-foot boat, but it had been raining since midnight, with no chance of letting up. It was not a good way to start the weekend. Bailey took her clarinet out of its case, carefully put the sections together and clamped a reed in the mouthpiece.

Mr. Skinner, the band teacher, had encouraged her to tryout for a solo to play during the next concert.

Bailey and Amber had played a clarinet duet "Frosty the Snowman" in Liberty Elementary's Christmas concert. Amber kept saying, "I'm so nervous. I'm so nervous. What if I forget my part?" Bailey told her friend that she could do it, and Amber didn't miss a note.

Their mothers clapped like crazy when the duet was over and Bailey and Amber took a bow together. That was when they were in fourth grade and just beginners.

Bailey was glad that her clarinet no longer sounded so squeaky when she played it. She liked the way the keys clicked when she pressed them and the mellow woody tone of the notes.

The only other person Mr. Skinner asked to tryout was a boy named Tim, who sat next to her. She put her mouth over the reed and slowly played a B-flat scale to warm up. There was plenty of time to practice because it would be at least an hour before Sugar was ready to go to town. She was in her office with the door closed. Bailey opened her band folder and propped up her part for a Sousa march on the chair she was using as a music stand. Shadow jumped on the chair, knocking the music to the floor. Shadow got into more trouble every day, and Sallie always followed him. Bailey set up the music again and continued practicing.

It was still raining hard when Sugar called, "Put on your raincoat. It's time to go."

Bailey had a new raincoat—new from a thrift store anyway—and dark blue pull-on rubber boots with green soles. The colors reminded her of the water at the beach i Florida. Sugar found the boots on sale at the farm co-op. "Mucking-about boots," said Sugar. "You'll need them. It can get pretty muddy here when it rains."

Bailey remembered the heavy rains and scary thunderstorms that often rolled in during the late afternoons of summer and early fall in Florida. As fierce as the storms were, they usually lasted only an hour or so. Then she often saw a beautiful rainbow, sometimes a double one, stretched high across the horizon. While there were still tall thunderclouds dotting it, the sky blazed with purple and orange, pinks and red, and the hot, humid air briefly cooled. Those were the times when she and her mother took bicycle rides on the deserted back roads and watched for rabbits, quail, armadillos and bobcats.

Bailey discovered that the Virginia rains could last for days, not hours. The dirt, the color of a new penny, became muddy and mucky and stuck to her boots like pounds of glue. She couldn't scrape all of it off her feet before she climbed in Sugar's truck.

"Don't worry, that's what the floor mats are for. Now then, always keep your eyes open for turtles, even in the winter," said Sugar, making the windshield wipers go faster. "This truck stops for turtles, even in the rain. They get in the road and then squash! I'll bet I've rescued a dozen of them in the last year. It's a little early for them to be out, but I always look. It's good practice," said Sugar.

"What do you do with them?" asked Bailey. "Do you bring them home?"

"Oh, no," said Sugar, with a laugh. "I give them a lecture about being in the middle of the road and put them well off the side, being careful to face them away from the road. They usually go inside their shells when I pick them up so I don't really know if they are listening. But somebody's got to tell 'em," she said. "You are now officially part of Sugar's turtle patrol."

Bailey grinned. Mom sure was right about Sugar's adventures.

10

Fix-up Party

Sugar was correct about the muck. Bailey's new boots became covered with what she called "goopy stuff" when she waded into the ditch by the side of the road to get the newspaper from its tube. The muck clung to her boots like giant wads of yellow gum. Sugar was out walking alone now that the rain had stopped. Bailey had decided to play with the kittens instead of going with her.

Glancing out the window a few minutes later, Bailey thought she could see Sugar coming out of the dirt logging road about a half mile down the street. The entrance to the road was blocked by branches, and there were yellow NO TRESPASSING signs tacked on two trees. The narrow, rut-filled road disappeared into the thick brushy pines. Bailey shuddered. The woods looked so dark and unfriendly that she couldn't imagine wanting to explore that particular forest planted by a timber company, even if the yellow signs had said WELCOME instead of NO TRESPASSING.

Bailey walked back to the front porch, stamping her feet to remove the goop. She was about to sit on the porch swing to wait for Sugar to return when she noticed another sack of trash dumped near the garage. She decided to clean it up while she waited.

She waved as Sugar strode briskly up the driveway, her red wool jacket unbuttoned. Bailey noticed that the muck on her brown work pants was way above the tops of her boots. She opened her mouth to ask where Sugar had been, and to tell her about the new bag of trash, but Sugar didn't give her a chance.

"I think we'll redecorate your room today," she announced. "The purple curtains and yellow paint just don't go with your new patriotic quilt. So, let's go get paint and material and have us a fix-up party."

Bailey had to admit it sounded like a good idea. She hadn't wanted to hurt Sugar's feelings, but the colors were pretty icky. It wasn't like her room at home with its pink-and-white checked curtains and floral wallpaper. Every-thing had matched, right down to the extra cushions on the bed. Her mother copied deco-rating ideas from magazines and home-im-provement shows on TV. She wasn't like Sugar, who seemed to buy everything, including tow-els and curtains, because they were cheap or on sale at yard sales. Sugar told her the dark yellow paint was there when she bought the house. She had no reason to change it until now.

"And," said Sugar, her eyes twinkling, "we'll go to *real* stores to get everything."

Bailey was secretly relieved. She was never sure where her grandmother intended to shop. Treasure hunts didn't always mean finding treasures.

Sugar made good on her promise. At the paint store, Bailey picked bright blue paint for one wall, and a snowy white for the others. At a department store she had never heard of be-fore, Bailey selected red café curtains with white stars for the dormer window.

Back at the house, Sugar spread out old newspapers to protect the beige carpet. She and Bailey put on big shirts that had be-longed to Grampa and their oldest jeans. Her grandmother showed Bailey how to use a small brush to paint the edges of the wall while Sugar stood on a ladder to roll paint on the upper part. Then she handed Bailey the roller and let her finish the bottom half, the part she could easily reach. Next they painted the other walls white, then stood back to admire their work.

"After the paint is dry we'll decide what you want to put back up. I've always had all the family pictures on this wall, but if you'd rather put posters up, well, it's your room now, honey."

Bailey said, "Maybe a couple pictures. Let me look at them." She knew she wanted Mae's picture where it had always been, and maybe . . . "I want *all* the Wild Women," said Bailey, much to her own surprise.

Sugar's eyes crinkled. "That's a great idea. Here's one of your great-grandmother, and Mae, of course, and me and your mother, and my aunts, Julia and Patricia—they rode camels in the desert when they were young women—and there's room for more."

Bailey wondered if her picture would ever be hung with the wonderful Wild Women of the family.

"Look at us," said Sugar as she moved the mirror back on top of the dresser. Bailey saw that both of them were covered with speckles

These pictures of the Wild Women are hanging on the wall of Bailey Fish's bedroom in Sugar's house. Which one do you think is Mae, the spy?

of blue and white paint. It was in their hair, on their noses, all over their shirts and hands. There was a blue glob, the size of a raisin, on her chin and a bigger one on Sugar's ear.

"Let's hang the curtains and then call it a day," said Sugar.

"It really looks good," said Bailey. It wasn't her real room, but she had to admit that if she was going to live at Sugar's house, this room was starting to look pretty nice. The red curtains went up just as the sun was setting behind the tall trees.

Before she went downstairs to eat leftover spaghetti, Bailey again studied the faces of the Wild Women at different ages of their lives. They seemed to have faraway looks in their eyes. Many had their lips slightly turned up into a smile. In one picture, Mae looked more serious, as if she was making a spy plan or watching out for the enemy.

I wonder what it would be like to have a real adventure of my own, thought Bailey as she turned out the light.

11

The Rush for Gold

Mrs. Dudlee returned the graded spelling quizzes after lunch. Bailey had been getting A's and B's in everything. Her paper had a big A written on it in red ink, and the words "Great job!" She would find out before the end of the day if she was going to play the clarinet solo in the spring concert. She thought she had done pretty well considering she hadn't had very much time to practice. Bailey was thinking about what she might wear for her solo when she realized that she hadn't been paying attention.

"Any ideas, Bailey?" Mrs. Dudlee said, as she stood near her desk in the second row.

"I'm sorry. I didn't hear what you said." Bailey's cheeks reddened. She twisted her hair and pushed it behind her ear.

"I said the class needs to pick something to study for our special spring history project. I'm asking everyone for ideas."

The boy behind her whispered, "How about dog faces?" Bailey could hear snickering from his friends.

Mrs. Dudlee continued to look at her. "You are pretty new here and have good ideas. What do you want to learn more about?"

"Gold mining," said Bailey, without hesitation. "My grandmother said that people used to dig for gold in this area."

The boys stopped whispering. "My grandmother says that people can sometimes still find gold in their yards," continued Bailey, "but we haven't looked yet."

Mrs. Dudlee wrote "gold mining" on the board, and looked around the room for more suggestions.

"Dogs," whispered the boy behind Bailey.

"Faces," said his friend.

A girl, wearing a fuzzy red sweater, suggested that they start a paper and visit the local newspaper where her aunt worked.

A boy with dark curly hair, said they should make models of Monticello, Thomas Jefferson's home near Charlottesville, and have a contest to see which model was the best.

Mrs. Dudlee asked for a vote, and to Bailey's surprise, most of the class voted for learning about gold mining. "I think this is a fine idea," said Mrs. Dudlee as she glared at two boys behind Bailey. They were about to be sent to the office. "Most people think that gold was discovered out west during the gold rush, but before then, Virginia was ranked number three in gold production in the United States," she said. The boys stopped fidgeting and made faces at each other.

"Let's make a list of what we want to learn and who we need to talk with as resources. And don't forget to ask your parents if they have ever found gold," said the teacher.

Mrs. Dudlee asked Bailey to be the leader of one of three class groups to work on the project. Her committee had to learn more about where the mines had been located in Louisa County.

The bell rang and Bailey scooped up her books and hurried to the band room.

Mr. Skinner was writing the names of the soloists on the board. Bailey held her breath and crossed her fingers. She hadn't realized until that moment how much she wanted to be picked. First he wrote the names of the girls he had selected to play a flute trio. A boy was chosen for a trombone solo. Emily's name was not listed for any of the trumpet solos. Bailey couldn't tell if her friend was disappointed or glad since Emily, like Amber, said she always became nervous when she had to play in front of people.

When will Mr. Skinner announce the clarinets? Bailey wondered as she twisted her hair.

"Clarinet solos," he wrote, and then turned to the class. "This was a hard choice since we had two very good players who tried out." He straightened his tie with pictures of saxophones printed on it. "So I've decided to let both Bailey Fish and Tim Snyder play alternate verses of the song and then do a duet on the third verse."

Bailey and Tim looked at each other and smiled. Mr. Skinner said, "Let's get started with our rehearsal. We've got a lot to do today."

Bailey put the mouthpiece to her lips. She couldn't wait to tell Sugar.

Even Justin's shout of "Florida girl, did you find your mother yet?" didn't bother her as much as usual. Bailey sat up front on the school bus with Emily, while Justin went to the back with his rowdy friends.

12

Sleeping Over

"Where *is* your mom? You never talk about her," asked Emily as the girls unrolled sleeping bags at her house. Emily's mother, a large woman with short yellow-blond hair was making pizza downstairs. Country music was playing loudly on the radio. Emily's little sister, Nannie, chewed on a pencil as she figured out her math problems. Her work sheets were spread out on the kitchen table.

Bailey smoothed out the green bag, something that Sugar had found in the attic, and put her soft pillow with a blue pillow case by the bag's opening.

Emily asked again. "How come you don't live with your mom?"

Bailey wanted to tell her new friend. She wanted to tell Emily that her mother was a

Wild Woman, off on an adventure in Costa Rica, writing a big article for a magazine.

But instead Bailey just said that her mother was on a trip.

"You couldn't go with her?"

"Nuh-uh. But we e-mail a lot."

"What about your dad?"

"He left when I was a baby. Hey, show me your DVDs." Bailey didn't want to answer any more questions. Emily seemed nice enough but sleeping over at her house wasn't the same as sleeping at Amber's. Amber knew everything there was to know, and Bailey could tell her everything.

Emily's mother, Mrs. Dover, turned down the radio and shouted that the pizza would be out of the oven in five minutes. It was time for the girls to wash up. Bailey could hear a man's voice.

"Dad's home," said Emily. "He runs a back-hoe and is a volunteer fireman. Do you like games?"

Bailey nodded.

"We can either watch a DVD or play games later. I've got a ton of them."

Bailey followed her friend down the stairs to the bright kitchen with a large round table near a picture window.

"Squeeze in between Emily and Nannie," suggested Mr. Dover.

Bailey looked across the table at Emily's five-year-old brother, Howie. He had a shaggy mop of dark blond hair. He smiled at Bailey, opened his mouth and burped loudly.

"Enough of that," said Mr. Dover. But Howie, still looking at Bailey, tried it again. He had been practicing burping with his friends during lunch at school. He had laughed so hard that juice had come out of his nose and he received a detention. His green eyes sparkled as he looked at Bailey for approval. She couldn't resist and grinned back.

Howie, his elbows now on the table, looked directly at Bailey and burped loudly again.

"Do it again and it's a time out for you," said Mrs. Dover, sternly. "We have company tonight, young man."

"Oh, brother," said Emily. "Howie, that's gross. Don't pay any attention to him," she said to her new friend. Bailey tried not to look at Howie because she knew she would laugh.

Mrs. Dover, trying to change the subject, said, "So Virginia is quite different for you. Do you miss your friends and Disney World?"

Bailey said, "We didn't live very near it, but I've been there four times. We actually lived nearer to beaches and the harbor. I e-mail my friends, but . . . "

"I hope you'll enjoy this area," said Mrs. Dover. "I suppose there isn't as much for kids to do in the country. No malls. No movies. You must think you've come to the end of the world. It takes time to get used to a new place."

Bailey said, "I don't know how long I'll be staying. So it doesn't matter, I guess."

Just then, Nannie, who was seven, reached for a second slice of pizza and knocked over her glass of milk. The river of white spilled all over Bailey's lap. Howie laughed like crazy and fell on the kitchen floor.

"Lordy, you children don't treat company very well," said their mother, as she handed Bailey several dish towels. "I'll put your clothes in the washer after you get in your jammies," said Mrs. Dover. "Then they'll be nice and clean for you to take home."

Bailey didn't feel like she was being treated badly. Howie was pretty funny, and Nannie was very sorry for making the mess with the milk.

"It's okay," she said to Mrs. Dover.

"Want to learn how to burp words?" Howie asked Bailey after supper.

"Sure," said Bailey. "I'll bet you are a good teacher." Howie took a deep breath and burped her name. She had never heard anything so funny in her life.

Bailey had seen most of the Dovers' DVDs so Emily pulled out her new favorite video game, Crazy Dogs.

As Emily got the game ready, Bailey asked, "Do you know Justin Rudd?"

"Oh, yeah. He's been mean to a lot of people," said Emily. "My mom said he is insecure. That's why he's a bully and makes fun of people. His sister, Fern, is Nannie's best friend. But Mom never lets Nannie go over to her house. Their dad is pretty nasty. Nasty! Nannie says he hits the kids."

"Can I play?" Howie pushed the door open to Emily's room. He was fresh from his bath and wearing his favorite Superman pajamas.

Emily was about to say no—she had had enough of his silliness at supper, but Bailey said, "You can help me move my dog."

Howie snuggled up next to her, as warm as her kittens. Bailey wished she had a little brother like him.

13

Pictures from Florida

From: "Bailey" <baileyfish@gmail.com>
To: jbs25@yermail.net
Sent: Sunday 1:45 PM
Subject: To Amber

Dear Amber: I slept over at Emily's house last night. She's pretty cool, but not like you. You are still my best friend. We played Crazy Dogs and had pizza. Everybody eats a lot of pizza here. She's in my class at school and we ride on the same bus. Sugar said I can invite her to go out in the boat with us next week if it doesn't rain. Sugar got mad at Shadow because he climbed her living room curtains and put some holes in them. She says it's time for them to go outside during the day and climb trees. Sugar was yelling "Bad cat, bad cat" but when he came down, he climbed the curtain on the other window. I was laughing so hard. I got your picture of Skippy. He is getting so big. Does your mom let him sleep in your room yet? I miss you so much. Bailey

The mail that day included an envelope from Amber with three pictures of her puppy and one of Amber and her mother at the beach. Bailey studied their photo. It showed a sand castle, a picnic basket and the red-and-orange striped umbrella that they always put over the green blanket spread out on the white sand.

Amber had a red plastic shovel in her hand and was scooping sand onto her mother's feet. They looked so happy that Bailey felt the biggest ever lump in her throat. She remembered how her mother's hands felt spreading sun lotion on her back before she and Amber ran into the warm Gulf. Sometimes the water near the shore would be cloudy with sand after wind had stirred things up, but many times the water was so clear that you could see the stingrays and the small fish that swam near shore.

She and Amber waded out with their foam "noodles" until the water was up to their waists and then they floated and splashed each other and watched the boys on Boogie Boards run and skid along the shore. They saw their mothers talking under the umbrella. Amber's mother had short, brown wavy hair and big sunglasses, and Bailey's mother, Molly, had thick dark hair that fell to her shoulders. She had sunglasses with blue, reflective glass, like a state trooper's. Bailey liked the way her mother tanned beautifully.

The sand was sticky. They brushed off what they could in the parking lot before getting in the van, and then took a shower when they got home to get rid of salt and sand. When she was really little, her mother would rub her with body lotion that smelled like roses and then she put on a giant T-shirt. Her mother combed out her hair, and made braids sometimes, and asked her to pick out three stories before bed.

The lump in her throat ached.

"Bailey, are you done with the computer yet? It's a beautiful day. Nice enough for a boat ride and a . . ."

Bailey suddenly realized that her grandmother had been calling her. She sent the e-mail to Amber, as she waited for Sugar to say, "and a new adventure."

14

Boating up Contrary Creek

"Make sure you dress warmly," Sugar said, as Bailey shut down the computer. "Even though the sun is out, finally, the lake can be chilly in late winter and early spring. It's not like those nice warm beaches in Florida," she said. "And here, you'll need a hat. The sun can be really bright on the water." Sugar plunked a red knit hat with a tassel over Bailey's straight brown hair that she decided to let grow. It was at an angle so that her bangs still showed.

Sugar wore a tan floppy hat with a big brim with a long string that was knotted under her chin. The string kept her hat from blowing off in the wind and landing in the lake. By the time Bailey finished dressing and making two peanut butter and jelly sandwiches at Sugar's request, her grandmother had hitched the little boat trailer to the pickup. Sugar tossed life jackets in the back, strapping them down with bungee cords so they wouldn't blow out on their way to the boat launch.

As she went down the front porch steps, Bailey saw her grandmother looking at what appeared to be a man's footprints in the mud. Sugar studied them thoughtfully for a moment, then realizing that Bailey was there, said, "Hop in."

Bailey was constantly amazed by what her grandmother could do, like hitch up a trailer. "How did you learn to do that?" she asked.

"When your grandfather got sick, he wanted me to be independent, so he taught me all sorts of things. You do what you have to do. Girls need to know how to use a hammer and boys need to learn how to cook and sew," said Sugar, as she headed down the highway. It would be a short drive to Lake Anna.

"I'll need your help when we put the boat in the water. You'll hold the lines—that's the ropes—so the boat doesn't drift away, while I park the trailer. Then, after I get the engine started, off we'll go."

Bailey put her hand in the water. "Yowee! Cold!" Wispy patches of mist were rising in little clouds off the lake. When she heard a bark-like honking, Sugar called, "Canada geese—that's their name." Bailey peered over the trees to try to spot them. The six large birds were flying in formation—five were in a straight line, and the sixth was off to one side.

Sugar walked briskly down the path from the parking lot with her thermos of coffee. Her boots made a crunching sound in the gravel.

Bailey saw her breath in the air not yet warmed by the sun. Her grandmother put two cushions that could float on the seats, lowered the engine's propeller into the water, adjusted the choke, as she explained, then gave a yank on the cord. There was a sputter.

"Fiddlesticks," said Sugar.

She yanked again.

Maybe she doesn't know how to make it work after all, Bailey thought, already disappointed. She really wanted to go for a boat ride.

But on the fourth hard pull, the engine started. It made a happy chugging sound. After the engine warmed up to Sugar's satisfaction, she said, "Now step in carefully and sit down on that front seat. The front of the boat is called the bow."

Sugar pushed the boat away from the dock and the little brownish-green boat parted the smooth water of Lake Anna.

Bailey saw a bigger white boat with fishermen in it in the distance near a bridge and large houses along the shore. Sugar said that at this time of year, they would pretty much have the lake to themselves.

As the little boat putted under the Route 652 bridge over Contrary Creek, Bailey realized that the sadness she had felt deep inside since she had moved to Sugar's had almost vanished.

"Where are we going?" she called to her grandmother.

"Up the creek as far as we can. I need to take another water sample. And then, if you are ready for adventure, I'll show you how to steer the boat. Pour me some coffee, will you?"

Steer the boat? That would be something to tell her mom and Amber about.

15

Taking the Tiller

At Sugar's direction, Bailey opened the two bottles about the size and shape of a cigar, reached over the side of the boat, put her hand in the cold water and filled each. She tightly screwed the caps on the bottles and gave them to Sugar who wrote on the labels and then put them in a padded thermal container. Sugar told Bailey they needed to take at least two samples from each spot where they stopped, just in case one spilled or broke. Altogether, they stopped at four different locations.

After they sealed and labeled the last of the bottles, Sugar pulled the sandwiches out of her jacket pocket. Bailey had made them with so much peanut butter and jelly that the edges of the bread were gooey, red and drippy. She was so hungry from being outdoors she wished she had made another one to split with Sugar. Bailey licked raspberry jelly off her fingers before rinsing them in the creek.

Sugar said, "I'm going to appoint you my official sandwich-maker. This is the best ever!"

Bailey was more pleased than she let on. Back in Florida she had done a lot of cooking because her mother was often home late from work. And she'd been making her school lunches for years, ever since she'd been in first grade. Her mother often bought cold cuts and let Bailey use as much as she wanted in her sandwiches. Molly didn't know that sometimes, when she was very little, Bailey would just make "bread sandwiches." She wouldn't put anything between the slices because she felt lazy. And then she would trade them for something better that other kids brought.

Bailey dropped a piece of crust in the water and watched a hungry fish grab at it as the crumb slowly settled toward the bottom.

Contrary Creek had narrowed. Bailey could almost touch the roots of tree trunks on the reddish banks of the shore. Bailey saw three deer standing very still where the water was too shallow for the boat to continue upstream. The deer glided into the woods when Sugar said, "Okay, time to head back." She turned the little boat around and motioned to Bailey to join her on the narrow seat nearest the engine.

Bailey walked carefully toward the back or "stern" as Sugar said the back of a boat was called. She didn't want it to tip over and dunk herself into the cold, cold water.

Sugar said, "Put your hand with mine on the throttle. Turn it a little at a time until the boat is going just the right speed. That's right. Turn it a little more. Good." Sugar removed her hand once they were under way. "When you want the boat to go to the right—that's 'starboard,' push the tiller towards your left. If you want to go left, or 'port,' push it to the right."

Bailey nodded. "It's just the opposite of steering a bicycle," she said.

"Now, see that gray house with the blue slide on the dock over there?" asked Sugar. "Aim toward it for a little bit. I'll tell you when to change course."

Bailey felt the warm sun on her face. She liked the way the tiller felt in her hand and the way the boat changed direction when she moved the tiller just slightly. Water rippled behind the boat, sending small waves toward the shore.

"The lake gets very busy on nice days, especially holiday weekends and during the summer," said Sugar. "A lot of people have vacation cottages or homes here. And then, there are people who like to camp and picnic at the state park. We'll go there soon. There are some good hiking trails. During the summer they let visitors see the ruins of the Goodwin gold mine and they can learn how to pan for gold."

The fishermen were no longer under the bridge. Once Bailey and Sugar had left Contrary Creek, Bailey could see two small sailboats in the main part of the lake and the boat launch was visible in the distance.

Bailey didn't want the trip to end. She was really enjoying steering the boat. "Do we have to go back?" she said loudly over the *putt-putt* of the engine.

Sugar said, "Well, maybe we can take a little ride, now that our business is done. Turn a little more to starboard and increase the speed."

The little boat seem to fly over the smooth lake. Bailey took off her hat so the wind could blow through her hair. *Maybe I can learn to be a Wild Woman*, she thought, *and maybe even have a boat adventure.*

16

Disappointing Trip

"So how's your gold mining project coming?" asked Sugar, as she chopped onions and peppers for a meat loaf. Bailey helped by peeling, washing and buttering the skins of two large baking potatoes.

"Pretty well. We have committees working on different things. My group has to make a map and locate where the mines were in Louisa County. Another group is looking into the process of gold mining, and the third group is supposed to find out about the lives of some of the early settlers in Mineral."

"How will you locate the mines for your map?" asked Sugar as she mixed the bread crumbs into the ground beef. "I've heard that some of the mines are now under the water of Lake Anna."

"I don't know for sure," said Bailey.

"How about getting in touch with the local historical society? They might have just the information you are looking for," suggested Sugar, patting the top of the loaf after she put it in the pan. "I know people who might be able to help you. And there should be resource books in the library."

"Thanks," said Bailey. "Do you know how to find the mine near Contrary Creek?"

"There were lots—about forty, I've heard—and the Rough and Ready Furnace. The Tender Flat Gold Mine was one near the Route 522 bridge. I'm pretty sure one used to be down that logging road that's about a half mile from here. Doubt there would be much left of it now. The mining here happened more than one hundred years ago. Mine shafts collapse. But sometimes you can see the stones from the old walls."

"Have you ever tried to find it?" asked Bailey.

Sugar didn't answer right away. "Well, I've been down that road a little ways. I guess not." She answered like she didn't want to talk about it further.

"Mrs. Dudlee said that if we do a good job we can enter the project in a contest," said

Bailey. "And maybe it will be displayed at the county fair."

Sugar said, "That sure would be nice." She had seemed a little distracted since she had opened mail and read another one of those reports from the laboratory. "It's not good. Worse than ever," she muttered as she read.

Bailey said, "Were those from the samples we took?" She felt proud that she was helping Sugar get information.

"Unfortunately, yes," said Sugar. "While the meat loaf is baking, I need to give Harry a call. I think it's time for us to take a further look in the woods."

Bailey heard Sugar tell Harry that the following evening they should meet at her house. His wife would stay with Bailey until they returned. "Bring your big flashlight," she said.

Bailey wanted to say, "Let me go, too." That's what a Wild Woman would have said, but she knew her grandmother would say no.

* * *

Bailey worked on her homework while Harry's wife watched "Wheel of Fortune" and "Jeopardy" on TV. Sugar and Harry had been gone only an hour. Bailey had never paid as much attention to the grandfather clock bonging out the quarter hours as she was doing now.

Shadow and Sallie were curled up on the couch as Bailey closed her science book and went to the window. It was too dark to see anyone or anything. Why didn't Mrs. Smith seem concerned? When her game shows were over, she changed to the Discovery Channel to watch a program about exploring the pyramids.

Bailey tried to concentrate on her math problems. She was worried that something terrible might happen to Sugar. What about bears? What if Sugar and Harry had been eaten by bears?

The clock bonged nine times. Where were they? Her homework was finally done and it was time for bed, but Bailey knew that she couldn't sleep unless she was sure that Sugar had returned safely.

Just then she heard steps on the porch and her grandmother's voice.

As Sugar and Harry came inside, her grandmother said, "Nothing. We found nothing. Nothing at all. I don't know where we go from here. It is a mystery."

17

The Hat in the Attic

"Florida girl, I think you need to sit in the back of the bus with me and my friends and tell us about yourself," said Justin, hissing softly so the bus driver wouldn't hear the nastiness in his voice. "C'mon back. We want to know what happened to your mama and your daddy."

Bailey looked out the window, pretending not to hear him. Justin moved to the seat behind her for the ride home from school. He wouldn't let up. "BaileyFish, I think you need to tell us where you got your name. Come sit in the back with us, Miss Minnie Mouse from Florida." The boys in the back seat laughed when he turned around and made mouse ears with his hands on the side of his head.

Emily whispered, "He's getting meaner and meaner to you. Have you said anything to your grandmother? Maybe she can make him stop bothering you."

Bailey shook her head and stared out the window. Justin finally returned to his friends. She could hear them chanting, "Bailey Fish. Bailey Fish. Bailey Fish. Where's your mama, Bailey Fish?"

She was very relieved when the yellow bus slowed down to let him off.

At the next stop, Bailey grabbed her books and bolted down the bus steps.

Was Emily right? Should she say something to Sugar? No. Sugar seemed like she had enough on her mind lately.

Bailey unlocked the door and went in. The house was empty. She had forgotten that Sugar had a dental appointment in town.

Before she started on her homework, she looked at the pictures of the Wild Women. Would they have let someone like Justin scare them or make them cry? Nope. She was sure of it. She wondered when they knew they were Wild Women and when they had their first adventures. Was Mae planning to be a spy when she was eleven? Maybe Sugar would know. She knew a lot of stories. Bailey looked in the mirror and practiced having a faraway look in her eyes and smiling like the Wild Women.

Then she remembered the hat. Sugar had told her that Mae's feathered hat was in a round red hat box in the attic. That shouldn't be too hard to find.

Bailey got a stool and reached for the long thin rope used to pull down the attic ladder. The steps creaked as they unfolded. "Don't come up here," she said firmly to Shadow and Sallie. Their faces were full of curiosity, and she could tell they wanted to follow her.

When Bailey reached the top, she pulled on another long string to turn on the attic light that barely lit the large unfinished room. She saw several mousetraps, numerous cardboard boxes, three rusty file cabinets, two old trunks, a rack of Sugar's summer clothes, picture frames, a full-length oval mirror on a wooden stand, a medium-size carton with the words "Molly's letters" written on it, and a round red hat box, just like Sugar had described.

Bailey untied the silky black string that held the lid on and opened it. Inside was Mae's dark green felt hat with a short black feather. Bailey carefully lifted it out, and put it on her head. She walked over to the mirror and studied herself. "I do look like a Wild Woman," she said quietly, as she turned her head from side to side. "A spy."

Still wearing the hat, she picked up the box of her mother's letters. She was about to open it when she heard Sugar's truck coming up the gravel driveway. She knocked on the attic window and waved to her grandmother as she got out of the pickup.

Before Sugar joined her in the attic, Shadow and Sallie decided to make the climb. They raced around, exploring all the corners and boxes. Their whiskers and tails were covered with cobwebs and dust.

"So you found Mae's hat," said Sugar. "Looks good on you, even if it does come down over your ears. Give it a few years and you'll fit into it."

"Does that mean I can have it some day?" asked Bailey, hardly daring to believe it.

"I can't think of a better person to inherit the hat," said Sugar. "I'll take your picture in it, and we'll send a copy to your mother."

"Sugar, how come you have a box that says Molly's letters?" asked Bailey.

"Wild Women tend to save things. We save letters. Before everyone had e-mail and used the phone so much, people wrote long letters that explained what was going on in their lives," said Sugar. "I have lots of boxes of family letters and stuff."

"Did my mother write about me?"

"Sure did. She told me about every tooth you cut, when you said your first word and when you started crawling."

Feeling bold with Mae's hat on her head, Bailey asked, "What about my dad? What did she say about him?"

Sugar sat down on one of the trunks. "What has your mom told you?"

Bailey said, "Not much. Only that he left us when I was really little."

Sugar looked thoughtful. She was quiet for a moment then said, "I guess there's no harm in telling. Your mom and dad married when they were pretty young. They didn't really have a chance to know each other. Your mother wasn't ready to stay home and do housework. She wanted to travel and to have an exciting career. He wanted her to stay home. They had some pretty big fights. Your dad, Paul Fish, joined the Navy. Shortly after he left, your mother found out that she was going to have a baby—you. Meanwhile, he met another woman and asked your mom for a divorce."

"Did he ever see me?" asked Bailey.

"Just once, I think. He sent money for awhile, but then nobody heard from him anymore. Your mother thinks he has a new family and they may be living overseas," said Sugar. "I haven't heard anything about him in years."

"Oh," said Bailey. Her mother would never talk about him at all. At least now she knew something.

"Do you have a picture of him?"

"I might. Somewhere. But now it's time to fix supper. What will it be tonight? Hamburgers or hamburgers?"

"How about hamburgers," said Bailey with a smile.

She studied herself in the mirror one more time, then carefully placed Mae's hat back in its box.

18

Milk Toast for Courage

"I'm asking for eleven volunteers," said Mrs. Dudlee, "to help some of the younger children with reading. We'll pair you up with first- and second-graders who need extra attention. It's sort of a buddy system. You'll get together during lunch hour a couple of times a week. Anyone interested?"

Ten hands went up. Mrs. Dudlee looked around the class.

"Bailey, I'd really like to put your name on my list," said Mrs. Dudlee. "You are one of our best readers."

"Okay," said Bailey. She had hesitated at first because she was still hoping that her mother would call, and she would be going home before the school year was up. But deep down she knew that wasn't likely to happen.

"Thank you all," said Mrs. Dudlee, writing down the volunteers' names. "I will be talking later today with Miss Moore and we'll get you all started by Friday."

Maybe I'll get someone cute, like Howie, thought Bailey. Although her friends, who had younger brothers and sisters always acted like they were a big bother, Bailey didn't think so. She thought they were lucky to have a bigger family and not be an only child. Even though Emily often complained that Howie was a brat, Bailey knew she liked him a lot.

Bailey was daydreaming about what her "reading buddy" would be like when she realized that Mrs. Dudlee was calling her name.

"Bailey, where are you, Bailey?"

"Sorry," said Bailey, blushing as the boys behind her laughed.

"I need to see you and the other reading volunteers just before school is out. By then I will have the names for each of you, and I'll tell you more about what you will be doing."

Bailey nodded to show that she was paying attention this time.

At the meeting, Mrs. Dudlee said that their job was very simple. They would take turns reading to give the little buddies more practice, and to help show them what fun books can be. "You can get some of your favorite picture books from the library, or encourage them to bring a reading book to lunch," the teacher said.

Then she went down the list of names. Because she was so new to the school, Bailey really didn't know any of the kids she mentioned.

Then it was her turn. "Bailey, I've assigned you to Fern Rudd," said Mrs. Dudlee. "She's a very sweet child and very shy. She needs a lot of special attention."

"Oh no!" Bailey gasped.

"What's the matter?" asked Mrs. Dudlee.

"Nothing," said Bailey. *How can I be involved with Justin's little sister? He'll kill me. Maybe I can get out of it. I just won't go to school tomorrow. I'll be sick,* she thought. *I'll have the flu. I'll pretend to puke. Sugar will have to let me stay home.*

"Bailey, you look worried. I know you will do a good job, and you just might make a difference. Fern really needs extra help if she is going to get into second grade next year. I'm sure she's looking forward to meeting you tomorrow," Mrs. Dudlee said.

* * *

By supper time, Bailey really was feeling sick. Sugar said, "Tell you what. I'm going to make you a special meal, guaranteed to make you feel better. It is something all the Wild Women ate when they needed to be brave, strong and well: milk toast."

"What's that?" asked Bailey, as she curled up on the couch

"Nice hot milk poured over toast. A little dab of butter. I think I'll have some, too."

Bailey was surprised at how good the milk toast tasted and that her stomach no longer felt fluttery.

As they were doing the dishes she said, "Sugar, did you ever have to do something in school that you didn't want to do?"

"Lots of times. What's up?"

"Oh, nothing. I signed up to be a reading buddy, but I don't think I want to do it."

Sugar said, "Why not give it a try, and if you really don't like it, then I won't expect you to continue. But you really won't know unless you try. Every day is a new adventure, you know," said Sugar.

Later, as Bailey looked at the pictures of the Wild Women, she knew they wouldn't have quit before they even started. "Okay, I'll try," she said to Shadow and Sallie.

19
Reading with Fern

Bailey was no longer surprised that Sugar had exactly the thing she needed somewhere in her house or attic. After they had mopped up the last piece of milk toast from the bowls that didn't match, she told Bailey to follow her into the library where she just happened to have books that first- and second-graders might like.

"I pick them up on treasure hunts," said Sugar. "You just never know when a little child might come to visit. I like to have things on hand for everyone. I also have a toy box in the attic. Some of the toys are ones you played with when you were a little kid," she said.

Bailey barely remembered those visits with Sugar when Grampa was alive, even though her mother gave her a picture of him smiling and carrying her piggyback.

"Here are some good ones," said Sugar. "I like this one, *Mrs. Rabbit's Lovely Present,* and this book of fairy tales. And here's one about kittens."

As she got ready for school, Bailey put the books in her pink backpack. Her heart was pounding at the bus stop. What if Justin knows? What will he say about it? Then the picture of Mae flashed before her eyes. Mae would be tough. She wished she could be like Mae. To her relief, Justin wasn't on the bus. *Lucky me*, thought Bailey.

When it was time for the first-graders to have lunch, Bailey was excused to go to the cafeteria. Miss Moore was waiting for the fifth-grade volunteers. One by one the older children were introduced to their reading buddies.

Bailey held her sack lunch and the picture books as Miss Moore, a plump, kind-looking older woman with her hair pulled up in a bun, led Bailey over to a small, blond girl with the bluest eyes Bailey had ever seen. "This is Fern."

Bailey said, "Hi, I'm Bailey and I have some books. Why don't you choose one that we can read together."

Fern looked down and picked at her green beans and burger.

Drats, thought Bailey. *She doesn't like me. What do I do now?* She decided to sit down and open her lunch anyway rather than go back to the classroom.

After a few minutes Fern said, "I'm not very good. I make a lot of mistakes. My dad says I'm dumber than dumb."

Bailey's heart melted. "We're not going to worry about mistakes. I made a lot of mistakes when I was learning to read. We're just going to read for fun. Hey, since this is just our first day, you pick a book and I'll read it to you. All you have to do is turn the pages. Then next time you can read a little to me."

Fern smiled and pointed to *Mr. Rabbit and the Lovely Present.* She moved her tray closer to Bailey, and said, "Let me try." Bailey listened to her read, helping the younger child when she stumbled over a word.

"I wish I could give my mother a lovely present," said Fern, as they looked at the pictures.

"Maybe you could draw something special for her sometime," said Bailey.

* * *

"How did it go today?" Sugar asked as she put some vanilla ice cream on the fudge brownies she had just baked from a mix. They smelled good, but, as usual, the brownies were burned around the edges by the time Sugar remembered they were in the oven. "Just scrape off the crispy parts," she said.

"Pretty good. I think my buddy can read better than she thinks. She just doesn't think she can," said Bailey

"Maybe she needs some milk toast for bravery," said Sugar. "What's her name? Maybe I know the family."

"I think you do. Fern Rudd."

"Very interesting," said Sugar. She was quiet for a few minutes and then said, "I'm sure she needs your help a lot. I'm extra proud of you. The weather is supposed to be pretty good tomorrow, how about another boat ride? It's time to take more samples from the creek."

Then she added, "If you would like to ask Emily to join us, we could pick her up on the way to the ramp."

As Sugar sat down in her chair, Bailey thought she saw that face in the window again. It glared at Sugar, then at her, before vanishing.

I must be making it up, thought Bailey, as she took the last bite of brownie. *It's probably just a tree branch that looks like a man.*

20

Another Boat Ride

Bailey was proud that Sugar let her take the tiller while Emily was along for the ride. After they had gathered the water samples and eaten their peanut butter and strawberry jam sandwiches, they headed back into the main part of the lake and turned southeast.

"What are those funny-looking buildings?" asked Bailey loudly over the engine noise.

"That's the nuclear power plant," said Sugar. "If it weren't for the plant, which was built in the mid-seventies, we wouldn't have this beautiful lake."

"How come?" asked Bailey.

"They dammed up the North Anna River because the power plant needed to have an impoundment area to provide water to cool the reactor used in making the power," said Sugar.

"After the water cools down behind the special diked area, called the warm or private side, it is returned to the main lake, which is called the cold or public side. That's the side we are on now. The water temperature can be fifteen degrees different between the two sides."

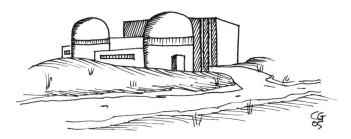

Bailey looked perplexed. "There's a visitor's center that explains the whole thing," said Sugar. "We'll go some rainy day soon. You need to know about the power plant. It makes electricity for thousands of people."

"Can I come, too?" asked Emily.

"Sure, and you can bring Howie and Nannie. They might be interested."

"You said that there were gold mines under Lake Anna," said Bailey peering into the dark water. "Can you see them?"

"No, they are long gone and the lake is more than eighty feet deep in spots. Virginia Electric Power Co. bought lots of farms in order to have enough land to create the lake. There used to be roads and trees, hills and buildings where the water is now," said Sugar.

"Now, Bailey, when we get near the bridge, any bridge, always slow down," said Sugar. "Then you can go faster again after we go under it, and when you are sure another boat isn't crossing the channel."

Sugar looked at clouds gathering in the southwest. "We might want to head back soon. I heard rain was forecast but thought it wouldn't come till evening. Looks like the weatherman was wrong again."

Bailey turned the boat around as Sugar had taught her the last time and aimed for the ramp area.

As she helped Sugar pull the boat out of the water onto the trailer, Bailey asked if Emily could spend the night. It was the first time she had wanted to have anyone over since she had arrived in Virginia, and she didn't know if Sugar would mind.

21

Temptation Strikes

"Does your grandmother always sing like that," asked Emily as she put on her lime-green flannel pajamas. Emily's mother whistled, but she had never heard her sing except on special occasions, like birthdays.

"Once in a while," said Bailey. "It is pretty loud. I think it means she's happy, but I'm not really sure. Sometimes she tries to sing along with songs on the radio. It's really funny because she doesn't know the words."

Emily bounced on the bed. "I love your room. And you helped paint it? You're lucky. Mom says I make too much of a mess. Who are these people?" asked Emily, pointing to the Wild Women.

Bailey explained, then told her about Mae's special spy hat.

"Can I see it?" asked her friend.

"I guess it's okay. Sure," said Bailey.

Within minutes, Bailey pulled down the ladder to the attic and Emily followed.

"Won't your grandmother mind?"

"Nah," she lets me come up and look around," said Bailey. She really wasn't sure what the limits were. Sugar had never said one way or another.

"Here's the hat," said Bailey, putting it on. She walked around like she was a model on a runway.

"Let me try," said Emily, she put it on her head and admired herself in the big mirror. "Cool! What else does she have up here?"

"Stuff. Plus she has a box of all the letters my mother ever wrote her."

Bailey was immediately sorry she had said that. It wasn't any of Emily's business. She knew Emily would be curious and have more questions.

"Have you looked at them?" asked her new friend.

Bailey shook her head. "The box is taped shut," she said. "See?"

"Let's look," said Emily. "After all, they came from your mother. You should be able to read your own mother's letters!"

The girls hadn't noticed that the singing had stopped. They didn't hear Sugar climbing the drop-down ladder.

"Showing off the hat? It's pretty old and very special so you need to very careful with it," said Sugar, as her footsteps creaked on the attic floor.

Bailey's cheeks were the color of strawberries. She was very relieved that they hadn't tried to peel the tape off the box of letters.

Sugar told them that one of the trunks contained photographs and Mae's scrapbook. "But I haven't found anything specific about spying, other than that certificate she received from the government for her service to the country," Sugar said. "Some rainy day we'll look through it if you're interested. Now, let's go back down and have a snack before bed."

Bailey wrapped Mae's hat in soft brown tissue paper and placed it back in the box.

"I don't mind you looking around, but there are things up here that are private," said Sugar, "so please just ask if you want to see something. Fair enough?"

Bailey said, "Okay."

Emily didn't look at either Bailey or her grandmother. She looked in the mirror and fixed the barrettes in her hair.

After Mrs. Dover picked up Emily the next morning, Bailey turned on the computer. There was an e-mail from her mother—the first one in more than a week.

From: "Molly Fish" <mollyf2@travl.net>
To: "Bailey" <baileyfish@gmail.com>
Sent: Saturday 10:53 PM
Subject: Good for you

Bailey dearest: Sugar tells me that you are helping a little girl with her reading and that you did a great job with your clarinet solo in the concert. I wish I could have been there but I'm clapping for you right now. Clap clap clap clap. By the way, I took a kayak trip through an estuary, which looked much like the mangrove creeks by the Peace River at home and heard what sounded like clapping. I asked my guide and he said it was giant clams, the size of dinner plates, snapping their shells closed. Maybe they were clapping for you. I hope you are making a ton of new friends. Write me back. Love, Mom

The concert, especially Bailey's solo, went very well, and Sugar was proud of her. As a special treat, they stopped for ice cream on the way home.

Her grandmother said, "Ice cream is not on my diet, but we need to celebrate!" Bailey knew that nothing was ever on Sugar's diet, but she always ate it anyway.

"Lick fast before it melts," said Sugar.

Even though the chocolate cone was drippy, Bailey didn't get any on her new blue dress. Sugar wasn't as fortunate. She had a large brown smudge on her white sweater. She laughed about it though. "I always spill something on this sweater. Never fails."

Later Bailey typed a short note to her mother. It was getting harder to think of things to say, with Molly so far away. Her mother didn't know what was going on every day like she did when they talked during supper.

Before hitting the send button, she typed:

P.S. Do you know when you're coming home yet?

She hadn't heard from Amber lately either, so she decided to send her a note.

From: "Bailey" <baileyfish@gmail.com>
To: jbs25@yermail.net
Sent: Sunday 8:20 AM
Subject: To Amber

Amber, I got to steer the boat again and Sugar said later today we are going to take a ride over to Charlottesville so I can see the Blue Ridge Mountains up closer. I rescued my first turtle the other day. I told it that it was bad for being in the road and put it in the bushes, just like Sugar told me. Gotta go. She told me to hurry up. Your friend Bailey

22

Reading Buddies

"What do you want to be when you grow up?" asked Fern as the girls ate the lunches they brought from home. Fern didn't have much in her lunch bag so Bailey offered her half of her own tuna sandwich, grapes and fudge cookie.

"I don't know. Maybe a spy. Maybe a teacher," said Bailey.

"A spy? That's pretty funny," said the little girl, as she licked the fudge frosting between the two cookie halves.

"I have a great-great somebody who was a spy. She was pretty cool," said Bailey.

"That's a lot of greats," said Fern, as she sipped her milk. "I don't think I have that many in my family."

"Whose going to read first?" asked Bailey, crumpling her brown paper sack.

"Me," said Fern. "I want to show you how good I am."

There were still a few words that Bailey had to help her with, but Fern was no longer afraid to sound out words that were not familiar, and Bailey helped her when she looked up from the book for assistance.

"Good job!" said Bailey. "You are really doing well."

"I don't know why my daddy doesn't like you," said Fern.

"I don't know why either. I've never even met him."

Fern went on. "He really hates your grandmother and calls her bad names. But I don't care. I like you anyway."

"I like you, too," said Bailey. "That's what counts."

As Fern reached for her milk again, her brown sweater rode up her arm a little bit. Bailey saw that there was a large purple bruise just above Fern's wrist.

"How did you get that?" she asked.

Fern quickly pulled the sweater over it. "I just fell," she said.

Bailey thought about the bus ride that morning. Justin had been acting funny lately. Ever since she had been assigned to help Fern with her reading, he had stopped speaking to Bailey. Not one word. No more nasty cracks about "Florida girl." Instead, he got on the bus, avoided looking at her and just walked straight to the back. She waited for him to come up to the seat behind her just to whisper something ugly, but he didn't.

That was odd, but it was a relief to have the taunting stop. Fern had never mentioned him so Bailey didn't ask. She thought she saw a bruise near his eye one morning. *If he hurt himself, oh well,* thought Bailey. She really didn't care what happened to him.

"What do you want to be when you grow up?" Bailey asked Fern.

"I want to be like you. A spy or a teacher."

Bailey said, "Maybe we could write a story next time about the teacher who was a spy."

Fern said, "Okay, I'll tell you the story and you write it down."

Bailey said that was a great idea, especially if Fern would read it out loud to her once they were done.

"Maybe you could draw pictures to go with it," suggested Bailey.

"For my mom," said Fern, with a grin.

23

What Would Mae Do?

Rain. Again. Bailey was soaked as she ran from the bus stop to her house. She found a note by the kitchen phone, where Sugar always left them for her. Sugar wrote that she was meeting with Harry and some other people. If she wasn't back by six, Bailey should set the oven for 350 degrees and put the chicken-noodle casserole in it.

Bailey opened a can of salmon-flavored cat food for Shadow and Sallie. They were eating so much more now that Sugar said they had the appetites of teenagers. Bailey half wondered if she should put their picture up next to all the Wild Woman. They were very wild kittens these days.

Sugar left a package of peanut butter cookies where Bailey could find them and put a note on the package that said, "Just two. Don't spoil your appetite. :)"

Bailey took three, as she knew Sugar would expect her to do, and went upstairs to her room, with Shadow and Sallie behind her.

She looked at the Wild Women as she pulled off her school clothes and put on her comfy lavender sweatshirt and jeans.

I'm so boring, she thought as she studied the faraway look in their eyes. *Bor-ring.*

She knew she had to spend time on finishing her gold mine report, which was coming together nicely.

Sugar had found someone from the historical society to come to her school to meet with Bailey's committee. He brought maps of where the mines had been located, and gave the committee copies to keep.

He talked to them about types of minerals that had been found beside gold—pyrite (fool's gold), copper, and sulphur ore—and shared with them articles he copied from an old newspaper. He told them that when the miners dug, they were looking for gold in its purest form. He showed them how the miners used pans to look for pieces of gold in the creek beds.

"Ore is a rock or mineral that contains a small amount of gold. Generally the ore needs to be washed, crushed, and treated chemically to extract the gold," he said.

Bailey liked looking at the pictures of the old mines with names like Arminius and Boyd Smith and learned that some of the workers, "nippers," "tailers" and "muckers," only earned $1.50 a day—a lot less than her allowance.

She and her committee wrote the man a nice thank-you note. He certainly had given them a lot of information for their report.

Sugar drove her to the library after school one afternoon where they looked up books on gold mining. They also visited the Mineral Historic Foundation's mining museum, which had ore specimens, mining tools and more pictures.

Sugar said that just for fun, she was going to borrow a metal detector from one of her friends and they would see if they could find any pieces of gold in their own yard, especially when it was time to plow a plot for the new vegetable garden.

But, instead of starting her schoolwork, Bailey finished the cookies and pulled down the attic stairs. Shadow and Sallie were right behind her. They loved exploring and romping around the piles of boxes.

Bailey put on Mae's hat. As she looked at herself in the oval mirror, the box that contained her mother's letters again caught her eye. Although it was in its usual place, it looked like someone had put it away in a hurry.

That's odd, thought Bailey. *It used to be taped closed. I know Emily didn't move it when she slept over. And I sure didn't touch it!*

Bailey went over to have a look. One end of the lid was slightly raised.

She put her hands on the box but then stopped. She remembered that Sugar had told her not to get into anything without asking.

The rain slammed against the window.

But maybe Emily was right. These were not just any letters. They were her mother's letters. Maybe there would be something in there for her, something that Sugar hadn't told her.

Bailey's hands reached for the box and stopped again.

Except for taking extra cookies, she hadn't disobeyed Sugar since she had arrived.

What would Mae do? Mae was a spy. Mae would open the box.

Bailey's fingers lifted off the lid. There sure were a lot of papers and letters inside in no particular order that she could see. There were cards. Birthday cards. Mother's Day cards. Postcards. Cards from Christmas packages. And there seemed to be two piles—one of older things with envelopes, and a newer pile with printed-out copies of e-mail.

Bailey was going to start with the older stuff when she realized that one of the e-mails was quite recent. It had last week's date.

It began:

From: "Molly Fish" <mollyf2@travl.net>
To: "Sugar" <sugarsugarr@earthluv.net>
Sent: Monday 10:35 PM
Subject: my plans

Sugar, I know you keep asking about my plans, and you have every right to be annoyed with me. You've been such a dear to take Bailey, and on such short notice. It really would not have worked for her to come along. I need time to find myself. How long that will take I don't know. I know it seems like I'm being irresponsible, but I think I've done the right thing by sending her to you.

I know this must be a bother to you since you have your own life and you are very busy. Kids this age can be a bore, especially when you are not used to having them around.

I know you will find the right words to tell her that she needs to enroll up there in middle school and to make a new life with you. I'll continue sending you checks to help out with expenses.

She's a wonderful child, but I don't think this is the type of adventure an eleven-year-old should be on. I won't be in touch for a few weeks. We will be traveling in the rain forest. Love, Molly

Bailey couldn't believe what she had just read. She studied the e-mail again. At first, she felt as sad as when she was really little and couldn't find her soft stuffed baby doll and had to go to sleep without it. And then the sadness turned to a knot in her chest that felt more like something hard and burning. Why hadn't her mother told her herself? *Why didn't Sugar tell me I was a bother?* she wondered.

She put the e-mail back in the box and closed it. A flash of lightning startled her. As she looked out the window, she could see Sugar's truck coming up the driveway.

Bailey carefully placed Mae's hat back in its box.

She had a terrible thought. *I wonder if Sugar is trying to get rid of me? Is that why she keeps asking when Mom is coming back? Maybe Sugar's sick of me, too. Doesn't anybody want me?*

24

The Plan Develops

The more Bailey thought about her mother's e-mail, the sadder she became. "Maybe if I weren't so boring, she would have taken me along to Costa Rica. Mae probably wouldn't have taken me either," Bailey said to the kittens after she had gone to bed.

Shadow jumped on her feet. "Ouch, cut that out!" Bailey wiggled her toes so he would grab them with his paws. It was a game they played every night. "Ow!" she said. "No biting. You're too rough!"

As Bailey teased the kittens with her feet she continued to worry. If her mother didn't think she was adventurous enough to live with her, perhaps Sugar felt the same way.

After all they were all part of the Wild Women of the family. Bailey needed to have an adventure of her own. Maybe then her mother would realize she was ready for a big adventure, too. Then it came to her. She quickly got out of bed, tumbling the surprised kittens to the floor. She turned on the lamp on her desk and looked through her papers from the historical society. In the middle of the pile was the map of the former gold mine locations.

She studied the one nearest to Sugar's house—the one on a tributary to Contrary Creek. If Sugar was right and the logging road led up to the former mining site, then Bailey might be able to locate it. Maybe she could find evidence of it to bring back for her report. She could prove that she, too, could be adventurous.

I'll have to find a time to go exploring when Sugar isn't around. She probably wouldn't want me to go in the woods alone, Bailey thought.

She decided to make a list of what she would need to take with her: Her backpack, heavy shoes, her warm jacket, knit cap and gloves. Also, a trowel from Sugar's set of garden tools in case she needed to dig, a pie tin to pan for gold, and something to eat. She tried to think if there was anything else Mae would have taken with her on a spying mission.

Bailey added double-fudge cookies to the list. She looked up at the picture of Mae and whispered, "I'm going to have an adventure of my own!"

After hiding her list in her desk drawer under some postcards her mother had sent, with pictures of sloths, toucans and iguanas, Bailey climbed back in bed. Sallie and Shadow were waiting for her, ready to resume their toe-grabbing game.

25

Spying Mission

Ever since she had made the list of what to take when she looked for the gold mine, Bailey felt better. She often took her homework to the attic where she would put on Mae's hat and sit in the dormer window. She decided to hide her notebook, where she kept her plans and observations, under the hat box.

She wrote: "Logging road." A good spy would notice little details about it.

On her way to and from the bus stop, she paid more attention to where it went into the woods. After a few days she was surprised to see that the usual branches and brush blocking the entrance, seemed to be moved. They were not always in the same place.

Bailey didn't think Sugar was the one who had done it because she had only seen her grandmother walking out of the woods a couple of times.

One afternoon Bailey rode her bike down to the logging road and back, just to see how long it took. It was about three minutes. She wrote that in her notebook.

She wanted to tell Emily about her plans, but was afraid her friend would blab to someone. Emily always blabbed. And, Bailey didn't dare e-mail Amber about it because Sugar might see the e-mail. No, this was Bailey's secret adventure.

Bailey also needed to find out when Sugar would be gone for a few hours so that she would have time to walk back to the mine, gather her evidence and return. But Sugar had no doctor's appointment and no trips to town scheduled in the next few days. Time was running out. The special reports were due next week. Bailey had almost finished writing her part of it and had made some charts and posters, but she really wanted to find evidence of the mine.

"How's the report coming?" asked Sugar as she fixed a salad, with lettuce, chopped green peppers and sliced carrots.

"I'm almost done," said Bailey. "Do you want to read it?"

"I'd love to, honey," said Sugar.

She sounded so genuinely interested and loving for a moment that Bailey wondered if she were wrong about Sugar wanting to get rid of her. But then her mother's e-mail flashed into her mind. Something was definitely going on that nobody was telling her about. Her mother had been really nice to her, too, just before she announced that she was sending her away. So how could she trust Sugar?

Her grandmother said, "Please set the table for me. Supper's about ready. Tomorrow after school we'll have a treasure hunt in Richmond. I need to stop at a few secondhand stores to look for a different kitchen clock because this old one has stopped working, and for gardening books. Maybe at the same time you can find some new books for Fern."

Bailey knew that aside from whatever it was that Sugar was looking for, they would always find something unexpected. Sugar told her that it didn't matter if they needed it as long as it was a bargain. On the last treasure hunt, she found four large flowerpots that she said would be good for planting pansies, a cast-iron skillet that was perfect for bacon, and the sky-blue lamp for Bailey's desk. On an earlier trip she bought a white wooden desk with bookcases for Bailey. It had three drawers on the left side and a concealed one across the center for pencils and pens. And on a trip to Louisa, she found the red bicycle for Bailey, and it was still shiny.

"Then, on Friday, I have to go to another meeting about the pollution. It starts at four o'clock so I'll have a snack out for you when you get home from school and instructions about putting supper in the oven. I hope you don't mind," said Sugar.

Bailey said, "I'll be fine."

At first when she had to come home to an empty house she hated it, even though she said she didn't care. Without Sugar there, the big house seemed very quiet. It made strange creaking noises that sounded like ghost foot-steps. Branches scraped against the windows when it was windy. She was getting more used to the sounds, but she had never looked forward to being alone until now. This would be her chance.

Sugar continued, "We've got some new ideas about the pollution problem. If all of us in our group put our heads together, maybe we can finally figure things out. I'm more and more convinced that the pollution is deliberate. Someone is doing this on purpose."

"How come?" asked Bailey as she put the butter substitute on the table.

"We don't know. It could be the work of a kook, or someone who wants to avoid dumping fees. It is just happening too often. And people around these parts know how to dispose of chemicals properly. I think it's someone who just wants to cause trouble," said Sugar.

"Someone would be that mean?" asked Bailey.

"Yep, there are mean people in the world. Not too many, but some," said Sugar. "I hope the meeting doesn't go on too long. Get your homework done early, and we'll take a picnic out in the boat on Saturday, if it is warm enough. There are lots of nice coves around the lake that we haven't explored yet."

Bailey only half heard what Sugar was saying about the boat trip. All she could think about was her spying mission to locate the gold mine. She was already imagining that she would find tools that the miners left behind, and gold nuggets everywhere. She was sure the ground would be covered with gold.

26

Into the Woods

Bailey had trouble concentrating in school on Friday. She dreamed of finding gold nuggets at the Contrary Creek mine site. She'd be able to fill her pockets with them. Then she and Sugar could go shopping in really nice stores, or they could take a trip to visit her mother.

Mrs. Dudlee had to interrupt her daydreams three times during class.

"Bailey, you need to pay better attention," her teacher said, "or I'm going to have to have a talk with your grandmother."

"I'm sorry," replied Bailey.

It seemed like she had been apologizing a lot lately for daydreaming. But sometimes her plans were more interesting than what Mrs. Dudlee or the other teachers were talking about in class.

The bus ride home seemed to take forever, especially when they had to stop at a railroad crossing for a slow-moving freight train. Emily chattered the whole way, apparently not noticing that Bailey wasn't saying anything. Emily said that Fern was spending the night with Nannie, and that her mother was going to let her make a cake from scratch instead of using a box mix. The best part was licking the bowls of batter and frosting. Her mother would probably make her share some of the frosting with Howie, who always hung around the kitchen when Mrs. Dover made dessert. "He's such a pain," Emily rambled on.

Bailey just looked out the window. She was still thinking about her adventure.

When Justin got off, he avoided looking at her, as he had done for several weeks. Bailey was quite relieved that at most he glared, but didn't tease her about her name or family.

When the bus passed the entrance to the logging road, just before her stop, Bailey saw that the brush pile had been moved completely away from the entrance and thrown to one side. While that puzzled her, she didn't think about it very long.

Finally the bus reached her stop. "See you Monday," yelled Emily, as Bailey waved, then ran up the driveway. She climbed the front porch steps, two at a time, and unlocked the door. She took off her shoes by the front door so that she wouldn't track up the carpet. Sugar had left a note for her in the kitchen. It said to start the oven by five forty-five and that she should be home by six or so. *That should be plenty of time*, thought Bailey. She put a handful of kibbles in the kittens' bowl and gave them fresh water, spilling some as she hurried. She would clean the litter box when she returned from her adventure.

Bailey raced upstairs and changed into her oldest jeans and favorite lavender sweatshirt and put on warm socks. Shadow and Sallie had followed her, expecting to play a game of "bird" but Bailey said, "Later. I have something important to do. Be good until I come back. No wildness."

She knew that this time of year it would start to get dark soon after five o'clock and she really didn't want to be in the woods after the sun went down.

She checked her list, and remembered that she needed snacks. With a final look at the Wild Women, including Mae, Molly and Sugar, Bailey rushed down the stairs. She put on her warm jacket, checked to make sure she had gloves in the pocket, put three double-fudge cookies in a plastic bag and headed for the garage where Sugar kept her garden tools.

Bailey found a trowel for digging, which she put in her backpack, then she remembered she needed a copy of the map. She ran back to her room and got it, hurried back downstairs, then put on her brown shoes when she got outside on the porch.

I bet it would be faster if I rode my bike, thought Bailey.

Bailey pulled it out from under the porch and walked it down the gravel driveway until she reached the road. Making sure there was no traffic coming, she got on and pedaled fast toward the entrance into the woods.

Sure enough, the brush was still pushed to one side, and she could see fresh tire tracks in the mud. As excited as she was about finding gold, the tire tracks made her nervous, as if the sun had just gone behind clouds. *Who is driving in the woods?* she wondered as she stared at them.

27

Bear

The air was nippy, as if it might snow later. Even with her warm jacket and fleece cap pulled over her ears, Bailey shivered as she looked at the yellow signs warning people not to trespass. She ate a cookie for courage. She decided her bicycle tires would get stuck in the mud road. *I won't be trespassing for very long*, she thought. *I guess I'll just walk.*

She left her bicycle behind a pine tree, where she hoped no one could see it. Bailey looked around behind her, and took her first step down the road. The woods were thick with what looked like spooky Christmas trees. The tall pines grew so close together that they almost blocked the sky.

Bailey walked carefully, trying to stay out of the real gooey muck. She discovered that it was easier to walk in ruts made by the tires because they had packed down the mud.

The woods were even quieter than her grandmother's empty house. She wished Sugar were along to sing. Bailey noticed that all the tread marks were the same. *Hmmm*, she thought. *It looks like the same truck is going in and out. I wonder why?* She looked at her watch, another treasure Sugar purchased for her at a yard sale. She had been walking for more than ten minutes.

To her surprise she came to a fork in the road. She hadn't expected to have to make a choice, and the map wasn't very clear about what direction to take to reach the mine. She decided to go to the right, because it seemed to have more tire marks. She ate her second cookie, wishing she had taken the time to make a sandwich. *I wonder how far I have to go?* She thought she heard the sound of branches breaking behind her. Sugar had told her that there were black bears in the woods, but Bailey had forgotten about them when she made plans to search for the mine. She decided she'd better eat the third cookie quickly in case the bear smelled food and came looking for it.

When she heard the sound of a truck coming toward her, she jumped out of the path to hide behind a tree. As she hurried, her foot caught in a root, twisting her ankle.

Behind her, the crackling of branches was closer and louder. Her ankle burned with pain. *I'm doomed*, Bailey thought, as she lay down on the cold leaves, closed her eyes, and prepared to be eaten alive.

28

Mysteries Solved

Bailey felt the bear licking her fingers as it got ready to take a bite. When she opened her eyes to have a look at the animal, Bailey screamed. It wasn't a bear, but Justin Rudd's ugly brown dog. Justin scowled as he knelt beside her.

"Don't hurt me," she yelled. "Please don't hurt me." Justin covered her mouth with his dirty glove.

"Florida girl, shut up. I'm not going to hurt you," he whispered. He was firm, but to her surprise, not snarly like he often sounded on the bus. "Promise you'll be quiet."

When Bailey nodded that she wouldn't make any more noise, Justin slowly removed his hand.

The truck rumbled closer.

"Be still," said Justin. "Stay down."

A black pickup, with large containers, as big as garbage cans, bounced past in the ruts. The windows were down and Bailey saw the driver. It looked like the same creepy face that had stared at her through the kitchen window on her first night at Sugar's house.

"Who's that?" she whispered.

Justin said, "My father. He's crazy mad at the world and crazy mad at me because I saw him get chemical containers out of the barn and put them in the back of the truck. And then he threw a garbage bag in. I asked him what he was doing, and he sort of went nuts and chased me with a rake. I thought he was going to kill me. He'd hurt you, too, if he had seen you following him."

"I wasn't following him at all," said Bailey. "I wasn't following anyone."

"I thought you were because . . ."

"Because what?" Bailey looked at Justin's face. He was scowling again.

"Because your grandma is a snoop and I figured you must be, too. My dad hates her so bad . . ."

Bailey interrupted, "Then why are you helping me?"

Justin squirmed. He looked uncomfortable with what he was about to say. "Well, Florida girl, when I saw how good you were to Fern—helping her read and all—after I was so mean to you, well . . . I just . . . But it doesn't mean I like you. . . . "

Bailey looked at Justin's face. He no longer looked tough, and she could see the bruise on his cheek. "What happened to your face? Did someone hit you?" she asked.

Justin didn't answer for a minute, then he said. "When Dad gets mad, sometimes he's rough on us. And he always wants to get even with people, like your grandma. Hey, what are you doing out here anyway?"

Bailey hesitated, then said, "I was looking for gold." She wasn't sure that Justin would stay nice or would go back to being mean, so that was all she told him.

"I heard there used to be mines back here," he said. "I never looked though."

"When I heard the crunching in the woods, I thought you were a bear," Bailey said. "Why did you come down this trail?"

Justin said, "BaileyFish, I was chasing after my dad's truck because I was really angry at him. I saw it turn into the woods, then I saw you park your bike behind the pine tree. I knew my father had come down this road to dump leftover chemicals from his job. He knows it upsets your grandmother. I think he has made several trips in the last few months, lots more this week. I don't know what I would have done if I caught up with him."

"He must be the person Sugar is looking for—the one who's polluting Contrary Creek," said Bailey in amazement. She tried to look at Justin's face, but he turned away.

"What are you going to do now?" she asked.

"I dunno. He yelled that I couldn't come home anymore," said Justin. "I don't even care about that. I've slept in the woods before, but I worry about Mom and Fern and the rest of them. He gets nuts."

Bailey said, "I've got an idea. Help me get out of here—my ankle really hurts. We'll go to my grandmother's house. Sugar will help you. She will know what to do."

"She might not like me because of my dad. Besides, he made me help him dump that trash in your yard," said Justin. He looked tired and his stomach growled loudly.

Bailey thought for a minute and said, "You can tell Sugar about what happened and tell her you're really sorry. But I know she'll help you."

Bailey looked at her watch. "Oh no! I'm really late. Supper isn't started and Sugar will be home soon. You've got to get me home. I don't think I can walk very well."

Justin helped her up and said, "Put your arm over my shoulder. I've been in these woods a lot and I know a short cut. Hang onto me and try to stand up. Okay, let's go."

"Owie!" yelled Bailey.

"Shhh," said Justin. "I told you to be quiet. I don't know where my father is."

Bailey whispered, "Ow! Ow! Ow!" as she tried to put weight on her throbbing ankle.

"That's better," said Justin.

As they got to the road, Bailey thought she could hear Sugar calling, and calling and calling her name.

29

Home at Last

As Bailey and Justin hobbled up the front steps, Sugar heard them coming. She opened the door, her face full of worry. "Where have you been? I've been frantic."

Justin said, "Please don't get mad at her."

"I'm not mad, but I was scared silly. What happened to both of you?"

Before they answered, Sugar said, "Let me see your foot."

"Ouch," said Bailey. "It's my ankle. I can't bend it."

Sugar had to cut off the shoelace because it hurt Bailey too much to pull her foot out.

Sugar said, "We'll probably drive into Fredericksburg to make sure it isn't broken, but first I need to know what you two were doing wherever you were."

Sugar fixed them hot cocoa in mugs that didn't match and let Bailey and Justin sit on chairs near the fireplace so they could get warm. "Now tell me the whole story. Everything."

Bailey fidgeted and looked nervously at Justin. "I'll tell you part now and part later," she said to Sugar.

"Okay," said her grandmother.

"The part for now is that I wanted to find a gold mine, to have an adventure. I saw a guy driving a truck—it was the same face I saw looking in our window the first night I was here," said Bailey

"What man? You never told me about a face." Sugar frowned and pushed her glasses up her nose.

"You were on the phone, and I . . . I thought I was making it up." Bailey saw that Sugar looked even more worried.

"And then I thought a bear was after me, and I fell, and Justin helped me home," said Bailey quickly.

Then Sugar asked Justin what happened to his face. The boy described how he had gotten the bruise. As Justin finished explaining, Bailey interrupted. "And Sugar, we know who is polluting Contrary Creek," she said.

"What? Who?" asked Sugar.

Justin said, "My father. I know I'll get in trouble for telling. He hates you for turning him in about the dogs and would do anything to get back at you. And we even saw his truck coming out of the woods. And I know he was the one who put the garbage in your yard because I was in the truck," said Justin. He stared at his hands, which he twisted and turned in his lap, then took a deep breath. He looked directly at Sugar. "I'm sorry I did that. He made me."

With a big smile, Sugar said, "Apology accepted. Stay put for a few minutes. I've got to make a few calls. Then we're going to town to get Bailey's ankle and your face checked out. And, since my helper in the kitchen forgot to start supper, I think we'll get a bite to eat on the way back."

They could hear Sugar first asking to speak to Justin's mother, and then she called the sheriff and finally Harry.

Bailey said to Justin, "I told you she'd help."

Justin leaned back in his stuffed chair and stared glumly at the ceiling.

30

Sugar's Surprise

Bailey sat on the front porch with Shadow and Sallie. Even though her ankle was taped, Sugar said they could take a boat ride later as long as Bailey was up to it. The doctor told her to take it easy for a few days. The warm sunshine felt good and Bailey thought she could see buds in the tall trees.

It had been quite a night. By the time they had gotten back from Fredericksburg, stopping for hamburgers and milk shakes along the way, the sheriff was waiting for them in Sugar's driveway.

He had already been to the Rudd place, and after talking with Justin's mother and his sisters, he had arrested Mr. Rudd for hurting the children. The sheriff said he would deal with the pollution issue later after they gathered more evidence from the Rudds' barn and truck, and visited the dumping site during the day.

"It's safe to go home now," he told Justin. "Your father isn't going to hurt you or your sisters anymore. Your mother can't wait to see you. She's been worried, too." Then he offered to pick up the bikes and give the boy a ride home in his patrol car.

Sugar and the sheriff talked on the porch for a few minutes while Bailey limped into the kitchen where her grandmother had told her to wait. She was still expecting a scolding.

Finally, she heard the door close and Sugar's steps in the hall.

"I'm sorry," said Bailey. "I didn't mean to scare you."

"I *was* very worried," said Sugar. "I accept your apology. Now, what is the other part of the story that you didn't want to tell in front of Justin?"

Bailey twisted her hair. She was having trouble finding the right words. Her grandmother reached across the kitchen table and put her hand over Bailey's.

"Okay, I opened the box of letters in the attic. I saw Mom's e-mail, and I thought you didn't want me to live with you anymore because I was boring. Mom thought I was boring, and

I'm a bother to you. So, maybe, if I had an adventure, you wouldn't send me away. I wanted to find gold," Bailey answered, not wanting to say one word of it. Her voice felt like it was caught in a trap in her throat. Sugar looked as if she were going to cry.

"Bailey, Bailey," said Sugar. "Don't you know how much I love you?"

Sugar jumped out of her chair, knocking it over, and came around the table and swept Bailey into her arms. "You are welcome to stay forever. I was just trying to get your mother to tell me her plans once and for all, so we—you and I—could make our own. It wasn't fair to leave everything up in the air. And she just wouldn't make up her mind.

"So your mom and I had some late-night arguments on the phone and by e-mail until she finally admitted she wasn't planning to come back anytime soon. That was all I needed to know. I have never thought you were boring or a bother. In fact, you have that Wild Woman, faraway look in your eyes."

Sugar picked up the chair and sat back down on it. "Now I have a couple of things to say. I want you to remember that my stuff is my stuff, and to respect that. And I will respect your privacy, too. Deal?"

Bailey nodded. "I shouldn't have opened the box of letters."

"No, not unless you asked. We could have looked through them together and I could have answered your questions," said Sugar.

"And second, and most important, I want you to know that you always have a home with me. Your mother may come back and want you to live with her. I know you would like that. No matter what, Sugar is always here for you."

"I love you, too," said Bailey with tears sliding down her cheeks.

Sugar gave her another of those big hugs.

"Now, wait down here for a few minutes. I'll go get your bed ready, and then I'll help you up the stairs. That ankle is going to hurt for at least a week."

Bailey was very tired from her adventure, but she no longer felt boring. Maybe she hadn't expected to find the polluter, and maybe she hadn't found the gold mine site, but she had had a good beginning as a spy. Sugar had said so . . . and in front of Justin. She watched the glowing embers in the fireplace. The remains of the log fire still warmed the room.

Later, as Sugar helped her into bed, Bailey looked at the pictures of the Wild Women as she did every night before she went to sleep.

Then, she did a double-take. "What?" she said out loud.

There was a new photograph on the wall. She looked again. It was her school picture tacked up next to Mae's.

"Wow! Thanks, Sugar," Bailey said, as her grandmother turned out the light.

"There will always be new adventures for us Wild Women," Sugar said.

Book Club Questions

1. What makes a place feel like home? Give examples of specific things Sugar lets Bailey do that her mom might not allow. Do your grandparents have different rules and expectations than your parents? Would that change if you lived with them?

2. Bailey admits she is a "worrier." What are some specific things she worries about? Which of these things were worth being concerned about? On what occasions does she tell Sugar she is worried? Do you think she is safe telling Sugar her worries? When should kids keep secrets and when should they tell a trusted adult? Give your own example.

3. Change is more difficult for some people than others. What things happen that help Bailey adapt to her new surroundings? What does Sugar do to help her adjust? What else might she have done?

4. What makes a family? Bailey is tempted to read her mother's letters before she has

permission from Sugar. Do you think she should have gotten permission first? Is it okay because they are from her mother? Is it okay to read the diaries of others without their permission? Might it be okay on certain occasions? How do our assumptions sometimes get us in trouble?

5. Why are Justin and Bailey able to help each other at the end?

6. How do you think Justin feels about his father being taken away in handcuffs? Pretend Justin has an uncle George in Chicago and have Justin write his uncle a letter about what has happened and what he fears.

7. What should kids do when other kids make fun of them? Should Bailey have told Sugar that Justin was being mean on the bus?

8. Are some friends better than others? What makes a friend special?

9. What should Bailey Fish do on her next adventure?

You can e-mail Bailey at
baileyfish@gmail.com
or write to her at
P.O. Box 544,
Mineral, VA 23117

Web sites
(Sites available as of press time)

Charlotte County
www.floridanetlink.com/charlotte.htm

Costa Rica
www.costarica.com/Home/

Gold Mining in Virginia
www.goldmaps.com/east/
Virginia_gold_mines.htm

Lake Anna Nuclear Power Plant
www.dom.com/about/stations/nuclear/
northanna/nanic.jsp
www.eia.doe.gov/kids/ (search: Lake Anna)

Lake Anna State Park
www.lakeannaonline.com

Map of Gold Mine Sites in Contrary Creek
www.infiltec.com/gold/contrary

Red Tide
www.mote.org~mhenry/chemfate.phtml

Spy Museum, Washington, D.C.
www.spymuseum.org

Town of Mineral
www.louisa.net/mineral/

Read more about . . .

Gold and mining:

Gold Fever, A. I. Lake
The California Gold Rush: West with the Forty-Niners, Elizabeth Van Steenwyk
The Next Bend in the River: Gold Mining in Maine, C. J. Stevens
You Can Find Gold with a Metal Detector, Charles Garrett and Roy Lagal

Spying and World War I:

Codes, Ciphers and Secret Writing, Martin Gardner
Harriet the Spy, Louise Fitzhugh
Spy, Richard Platt
The Short and Bloody History of Spies, John Farman
True Stories of the First World War, Paul Doswell
Women Who Spied, by A. A. Hoehling

Glossary

dormer: A window projecting from a sloping roof.

furnace: An enclosed structure in which heat is produced for reducing ore.

impoundment: A body of water confined in a reservoir.

panning: To wash material such as earth or gravel in a pan in search of gold.

pyrite: A common mineral, iron sulfide, which is commonly called fool's gold, burned in making sulfur dioxide and sulfuric acid.

red tide: Seawater discolored by a large number of dinoflagellates or algae, which produce a toxin poisonous to many forms of marine life.

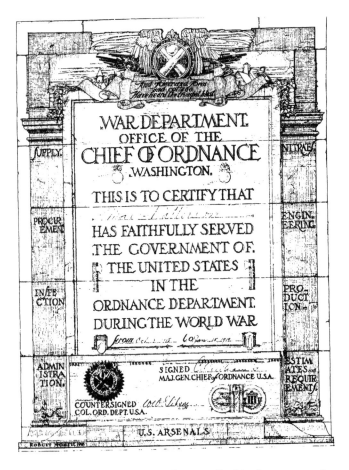

Words above the text in the scroll: *"And tower and town and cottage have heard the trumpet blast."*
War Department office of Chief of Ordnance
Washington
This is to certify that Mae Patterson has faithfully served the government of the United States in the Ordnance Department During the World War from Oct. 8, 1918 to Jan. 15, 1919.

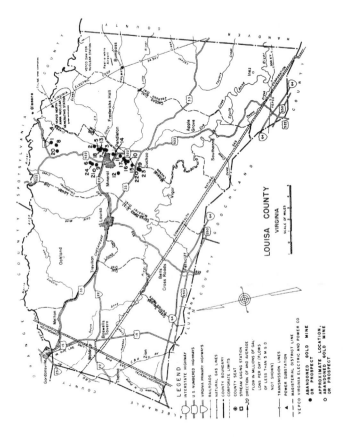

Black dots show locations of abandoned gold mines in Louisa County near Mineral and Contrary Creek. From Gold in Virginia, *Publication 19 of the Virginia Division of Mineral Resources*

Arminius Mine in Mineral, Virginia. This mine, which employed more than 300 men, was the deepest of the mines at 1,250 feet. Pyrite was its primary mineral.

ALLIE COOPER MINES NEAR MINERAL VA.

Allah Cooper gold mine near Mineral.

Both postcard pictures are used by permission of the Mineral Historic Foundation.

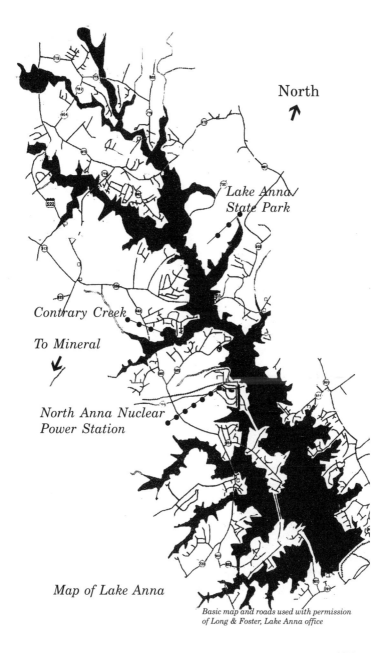

North

Lake Anna
State Park

Contrary Creek

To Mineral

North Anna Nuclear
Power Station

Map of Lake Anna

Basic map and roads used with permission
of Long & Foster, Lake Anna office

153

Acknowledgments

Many thanks to those who read and offered suggestions during the book's various stages: Joann Winkler, Charlotte County Teacher of the Year; Dr. Gaynell Whitlock, president of the Mineral Historical Foundation; Abigail Grotke, Elizabeth Madden, Jim Salisbury, Nancy Wettlaufer, Chris Grotke, Lise LePage, Ben Freivogel, Allison Hartsoe, Lola Casey and Nancy Miller, who developed discussion questions.

I'm also indebted to Patricia Seif who shared our relative Mae Patterson's story, and Mae's certificate from the War Department. Mae was a school principal in Piketon, Ohio, who quit her job in 1915 when the school board would not pay her as much as a man. Mae traveled extensively and after the war became a teacher of English and Modern History.

And to Julia Stallings, and Amberlyn Freidel for special inspiration.

About the Author

 Linda Salisbury draws her inspiration for the Bailey Fish series from her experiences in Florida and Central Virginia, and as a mother, mentor, former foster mother and grandmother.

She is a former newspaper editor and columnist, writes book reviews and articles for various publications. She is the author of seven other children's books.

She enjoys playing music and boating on Lake Anna and up Contrary Creek with her husband, Jim. They share their home with old lazy cats.

About the Illustrator

 Artist Christopher Grotke of Brattleboro, Vermont, is the creative director for MuseArts, Inc. He is an award-winning animator and has been featured in a number of publications, including the *Washington Post* and *New York Times,* and his work has been seen on PBS's "The Creative Spirit."

He has done illustrations and drawings for five books in the series, among others. He has two adventurous cats.